Felix Andy

lesbian fuck girls

Alien story

Contents

1

STIRRED

Chapter 1 STIRRED

The island has forever been uninhabited. Left in one piece by men and the immense high rises, he had the option to hold his regular magnificence. The leaves were more rich than any other time in recent memory. Blossoms of various varieties were plentiful, dissipated over the grass. In the event that you looked sufficiently, you could see a deer stowing away against the shrubs, or perhaps play with different creatures.

The serene existence of the island was quickly upset as three characters looked through the spot. They moved with such speed and power that an ordinary person wouldn't have the option to recognize them between the breeze. It required just thirty minutes for the island visitors to clear the whole region and find what they were searching for.

One of the island's inhabitants, a deer, inquisitively checked out at the three characters behind the brambles. He saw nothing other than different creatures, and he felt a sprinkle of energy and dread about the thing planned to occur. The deer noticed the three figures, all of which had a place with entrancing young ladies. One of them has kindled red hair, and a look that appeared to compare to the savagery of its strands.

Another young lady had a more pleasant face and a skin washed in sun. His eyes were more modest, in spite of the fact that there was delicate quality there. The two of them took a gander at the third, who appeared to be their chief. This young lady was unique. More forcing with determined height. With pale hair and eyes of dusk tone, she was more ethereal than some other animal. She was the sun.

"Do you feel that?" she told different young ladies. "This is where I pick the odd energy."

The female with red ostentatious hair examined the region. She originally looked at the sky and afterward really look at between the trees. Her look arrived on a deer concealing on the brambles, until she saw her partners. "I feel it as well, goodness Extraordinary."

Simon, I advised you to call me by my human name while we are here on the planet," said the young lady according to the dusk. "Carry on like people. Talk like people. Seem to be a human."

"Sorry Zeus ," Simon said in a conciliatory sentiment before she kneels.

Zeus cleared his conciliatory sentiment with a token of his hand. "diva ," she says. The young lady with tan skin got consideration. "Supplant this spot. I maintain that you should cautiously search for every one of the subtleties we could have missed. Assuming that anybody sees something, call me."

"Indeed Zeus ."

The deer kept on watching the three females quietly until they arrived at a big stake in their mission. One of the young ladies called diva requested the consideration of others. They saw an abnormality on the ground. The ears of the deer of interest. Different creatures have forever known about this anomaly, albeit none have had the boldness to research it further. In any case, the three young ladies were unique. They needed to search for him.

There is something on the ground," Zeus said. She stomped on her boots, as though she was trying the empty. "Simon, remove the soil and see what you can find."

The floor shuddered. It was a slight thunder from the outset. The deer nestled into its concealing spot as the shakes strengthened. Simon with blazing hair lifted his hands. As it did, a piece of the dirt was taken out, uncovering a hole formed shape that has never been there. The shaking halted. It required some investment before the deer quit shaking and might have taken the boldness to look.

Simon the huge piece of earth as an afterthought. It arrived with a dull clamor, flying more birds every which way as they escape to save their lives. "Is that what I think it is?" She asked then that she inclined to look with others.

"It's certainly a case on our planet. A rest container." diva talked. She was all around as energized as the two young ladies. "Would it be a good idea for us we investigate?" She hung tight for Zeus 's endorsement prior to moving. Each of the three bounced underneath.

The deer, needing to see what was happening, pondered to draw nearer to the young ladies or remain in the security of the shrubs. The visitor on the island didn't appear to be terrible animals, despite the fact that deer realized they could be hazardous. By the by, deer has seen nothing like this before in its long life on the island. With a striking race, he emerged from the shrubberies and went directly to check the pit out. He found the three females opening an oval-formed create.

The container, as the young ladies called it, delivered a steam when the top opened. Zeus and the others needed to stand by a couple of moments before the fume vanished. Simon pushed the more extensive cover, permitting them to see what was inside. "I can barely handle it!" she was panting. "That is balica . What is she doing here? Zeus pushed Simon automatically to the side in his scramble to look nearer. She became paler by taking a gander at the female's rest shape on the case.

"Have we at long last tracked down balica after so long?" diva inquired.

Zeus shut his eyes. "Something's off-base here."

"We should accept it above," Simon advertised. diva gestured and pulled Zeus away from the hole. The last option generally had a befuddled look as they trusted that Simon will take care of his business. The deer scoured from where it came from. He saw with enormous eyes as plants showed up starting from the earliest stage conveyed the container and Simon up close to the Zeus and diva pausing.

Zeus looked again at the resting young lady in the case. Her eyes were delicate as she brushed her fingers on the pink lips of the female. "There's something off-base," she murmured.

Simon remained close to Zeus . "What's going on here? Could it be said that you are glad that we at long last tracked down it? She vanished around 90 days prior with her dearest companion rashin and hasn't been seen since. We as a whole heard the news, but…"

"Simon," censured diva . "This news isn't correct. balica wouldn't do that. balica is a decent individual." She strolled towards them and put a hand on Zeus 's shoulder. "Obviously the news is off-base." She highlighted the resting young lady. "How might balica do these things while she's resting here constantly?"

"I wish it was valid, however this young lady isn't balica ," Zeus said.

Simon looked at their chief with addressing. "She seems to be Balica to me, not that I challenge your judgment Your Elegance. What is your take of it?"

Zeus kept on touching the dozing young lady's hair, as she did over the course of that time. "Her appearance is like that of my lady of the hour, yet some way or another I feel something else from her. Like assuming it were balica , at this point she's not her. The embodiment isn't like her."

"Well. Indeed, there's just a single method for knowing it. How about we wake it up," says Simon. "So we'll truly be aware on the off chance that she's Balica or not. "Zeus appeared to be questionable. "Simply sit back and relax," Simon said cheerfully. "diva and I are here, Mr Pioneer. We will uphold you as usual."

"OK." Zeus brought the young lady's hair down to her shoulder. She faltered before delicately tapping the young lady. "balica ? Awaken. "It stepped through a couple of exams before the young lady woke up, squinting gradually and didn't appear to see her watchers. "Hello," Zeus said, catching the young lady's consideration.

The deer could plainly see his response from where he was stowing away. The female's eyes enlarged. He plunked down in a rush and looked around him, as though he were lost. She propelled herself out of the case and rose up to crash. Zeus got her with two hands and took the young lady back to the situated position. "Balica , it's me, Zeus ."

The young lady opened a wide mouth, however no clamor emerged. She squinted her eyes and opened her mouth more extensive. She was murmuring however didn't let out the slightest peep. Disappointed, she got out of the throat and hacked. "Tell me," Zeus said once more. "What's happening?" Zeus investigated Simon and diva . "His pulse is expanding, however aside from that, his important bodily functions are ordinary, do you suppose something is hindering his aviation routes, keeping him from talking?"

diva stooped close to the container. She checked the young lady out. "I don't believe she's in harm's way, assuming that you're not kidding," she told Zeus . "I simply believe she's confounded."

Simon inclined towards the young lady. "Hello." She broke her fingers a couple of centimeters from the young lady's face. "How about you talk? You alarm our chief. You have been away for a really long time and presently you play the fool. "

Zeus gave Simon an admonition. "Stop it."

Simon promptly drew his hand. "However, I'm not used to seeing her like that. Regularly, Balica will return to me for being inconsiderate, or she will take steps to kick me. It's truly not the same as her." Simon was gasping. "Gracious, I know, I'll prod her somewhat more. Perhaps she will come." Simon got back to the young lady. "Hello, Balica . Do you have some scissors? Since that is the nearest method for making scissors. You grasp it? Ha." She glared when the young lady didn't respond. "Could she at any point try and figure out us?"

Zeus 's eyes sparkled when she went to the young lady. "Do you have any idea who I'm?" She didn't get a response. "Do you comprehend what I say?" The young lady saw her in white.

"There is by all accounts an issue with his discourse," diva said.

"I know," Zeus concurred. "That's what I'll fix." She shut her eyes and put her palm on the young lady's brow.

"I know," Zeus concurred. "That's what I'll fix." She shut her eyes and put her palm on the young lady's temple.

The principal felt that struck a chord was the warm word. Some way or another I realize that the hand laying on me was warm. I didn't have the foggiest idea how I knew it. I just knew it. I opened my mouth for seemingly the 10th time today. "Hot," I say. Indeed, that's what I intended, yet the sound that came out was "Wam", rather than "Warm".

"Once more, you talk," said one young lady. She had orange-shaded eyes, which brought me back from the word I began, warm.

"Hoo aw yoooo?"

The young lady hauled her hand out of my temple and fixed the other two. "Balica says the words like a youngster," she said. "I involved my power for his jargon, however such being is not assumed."

"It gets peculiar from one moment to another," said one more young lady with red hair. She confronted me. "Alright, we should explain that before I return. I'm simon." She contacted her chest. "This lovely young lady who looks Asian is my better half, and the person who is close to you is our boss, Zeus . You are Balica , our companion. You figure out it? You bailed us months prior. We searched for you, we tracked down you, and presently you act like a juvenile simpleton."

"simon," says Zeus . "Enough."

"I'm not Balica . balica is the girrrrl in my dweems." I contacted my head. "My dweems." How could I know these terms? How could I try and talk?

Simon feigned exacerbation. "Goodness extraordinary, she's not youthful, she's brimming with cuckoo, I'm trusting the evidence speak for itself."

"Where were you before that?" diva inquired. I mulled over everything. Where was I, she inquired? No place. I was no place else than here. I opened my eyes a couple of seconds prior and here I am checking out at the young lady with orange eyes. I shook my head at diva . She looked at Zeus and Simon. "She doesn't vaguely recollect

9

anything," she murmured. "I read about it in a book, I saw it on the show as well, and they said it was amnesia."

An insightful look crossed all over. "You say Balica vanished three months prior with rashin , had a mishap, lost memory and some way or another wound up on a uninhabited island with only creatures, and was put underground inside a case, the likelihood that this would happen is under 0.01 percent."

simon grinned. "Assuming you may, Your Excellency. People have said that life on another planet is not exactly the chance you recently gave, however we are right here. "

"However we are right here," emulating diva . Rather than contending with them, Zeus unfastened his sack and took something. "Did you bring your tablet?" diva inquired. "What for?"

Zeus squeezed to a great extent. "I changed the gadget to be cautioned at whatever point there is news from balica , I utilize the Earth satellite to have an association any place we go." She slipped the tablet. "Another glimmer came seconds ago." She zeroed in on the screen briefly prior to pushing the tablet inside the sack. "The news said they had seen balica some place in Brazil, and the depiction matched her."

"So who is?" simon went to me. "In the event that she's not Balica , then, at that point, who is she?"

Zeus contacted my arm. This made a rush stream along my spine. It was whenever I first felt that. Whenever I first felt anything. "Might you at any point help me out and isolate you from your hair?" she inquired. I did it beyond a shadow of a doubt while each of the three checked my temple out. "She has balica 's tattoo," Zeus said. "Be that as it may, I'm almost certain the balica they portray on the news likewise got a tattoo."

"Indeed," diva acknowledged. "Likewise, balica on the news is some of the time spotted with rashin ."

"Twins?" simon proposed. "That is the main clarification."

"In any case, how could the two of them have tattoos on their brows?" diva said. "Recollect that our species was brought into the world with a tattoo to show us who our perfect partner is, regardless of whether balica and this young lady are twins, they shouldn't have matching tattoos since it would imply that Zeus is intended to be with them both."

Zeus shifted my face toward him. "Are you certain that is no joke?" She asked me.

"Promise."

She moaned. "Then we will deal with you like his twin. What's your name? »

I shrugged my shoulders. "I don't have a canine."

"Goodness my kid," mumbled simon. "She resembles an infant, have you at any point been outside this container?"

"No. I awakened today."

Zeus looked through the prompt climate until his eyes arrived on a bloom. She ran there and was promptly close to me once more, as though she wasn't moving in any way. She gave me the bloom. "You are basically as lovely as this blossom," she said.
    "Flowa," I rehashed.

"Indeed… What's more, yes. Blossom. She goes by musi ."

"musi ," I said.

"Right. Treat you so harshly as that name? I looked at him and gestured. "Then, at that point, from here onward, we will call you musi , after this bloom."

"Incredible, we even name the child," simon said mockingly. "The before you know it is that we need to purchase diapers to dispose of any crap."

"Try not to be mean," diva criticized. "She is our child now. You can show him anything."

Simon's eyes illuminated. "Anything?" She jeered. "Goodness, you're hanging tight for musi . I will show you such a lot of that when I'm finished with you, you'll be perfect."

Zeus helped me. My legs fell, however she upheld me prior to getting me in her arms. "You're not as yet steady," she said. "I will help you." She looked at her sidekicks. "Prepared our boat. We will leave. Then, at that point, following a couple of days, we will proceed with our pursuit with Cairo ." She turned around to me as she conveyed me toward the path she needed. "Also, just to expose it, your twin found something important to her, which is the reason she vanished."

"What?" I inquired.

"She's an alien . And that implies you are as well."

2

ILLUSTRATION

Chapter 2. ILLUSTRATION

Welcome to your new musi home," diva said. She stood aside to give me access prior to shutting the entryway behind us. "This is your twin sister's condo. At the point when Simon, Zeus and I came to Earth, it turned into our home as well. Also, presently it depends on you. Indeed, basically until Cairo returns and fixes things." I looked as diva made sense of what each room was for. "Coincidentally, this is the parlor. Presently, what have you been shown on the way here? »

"The loom is where you acknowledge visitors," I answered.

She applauded. "Indeed, believe it or not. You learn musi rapidly."

Simon remained close to us with a fulfilled grin all over. "It's such a ton more straightforward to show him the best things throughout everyday life," she said.

"Simply ensure that what you will show him is worth the effort," Zeus said behind us. "Something she can utilize when we as a whole re-visitation of our planet." Zeus 's look changed in my course. He contacted my face for a couple of moments before she took her eyes off and left. "I will go to my room," she said. "Show him the nuts and bolts first." She vanished behind an entryway.

In the mean time, Simon pushed diva before me. "I'll pass on the exhausting things to you," Simon said. "I will initially take a delight rest. Not that I really want it. Being an outsider like us is awesome." She walked around another room, letting diva and I be.

"I get it ultimately depends on me then, at that point," diva murmured. "We should sit on the musi couch."

When we were perched on the cream-shaded couch, diva began getting clarification on pressing issues. She's been doing it for two days since we left the island where I awakened. They said my jargon was great, yet since my language wasn't accustomed to discussing words yet, I would keep on seeming like a kid.

Aside from that, they let me know that despite the fact that I knew the significance of the words, I expected to encounter it myself. They showed me the idea of varieties, time, numbers thus considerably more as we voyaged. Steadily, I started to figure out my general surroundings, despite the fact that I was unable to get a handle on certain things, similar to why Zeus helpfully stayed away from my twin sister's subject, and why her eyes had a far off look when balica was referenced.

"All you need to ask me consequently?" diva said.

"What is walien?"

"Gracious… You heard that from simon huh? I gestured. She tapped her jaw prior to replying. "All things considered, an outsider is what people call us." I scowled at him. Huh? diva got up before I could ask further. "Stand by there," she requested.

diva returned in no time flat, carrying with her few white things she called paper, and a dark barrel shaped object that she depicted as a marker. She slipped close to me and put the heap of papers on her lap. She attracted a little circle the center. "This is the Earth," she said. "The couch we are perched on is situated in a condo. The condo is in a city. The city in a state. The state in a country. The earth," she expresses, highlighting the circle. "Is comprised of nations with rules."

"Wules," I rehashed. "Standards or set of guidelines that should be observed."

"Right. And this multitude of nations with rules and so forth are situated on The planet. The species that involve the earth are called people."

"A lot of homophobic dolts, you mean," simon said distinctly from his room.

"Hello, don't instruct him that," diva whined. She went to me cheerfully. From my perception, simon generally prodded diva , in the event that prodding was what you called squeezing somebody's butt cheek region or gnawing her arm. Zeus said it was prodding, and simon got a kick out of the chance to do it with diva , albeit the last option delighted in it especially as Zeus would agree.

"In any case," diva said, intruding on my viewpoints. "People accepted they were the only ones known to mankind, yet as a general rule." She drew a few different circles close to the earth, and a bigger circle on the edge of the paper. "There are a lot more animal categories. People call different species outsiders. You, me, Zeus , simon, our other companion nash , lastly, your twin sister are outsiders. Yet, for people, we are not genuine."

"Why?" I inquired.

She shrugged. "Since it's simpler to trust that you're separated from everyone elsc in thc univcrse than to acknowledge the idea that a few animal varieties are superior to you."

At that point, simon emerged from his room bringing a rectangular-formed object. She felt free to sit on the floor happily. "Check this musi out. This gleaming thing is known as a tablet." She squeezed a button in the center. "It has a screen and everything. Presently this screen is where all the wizardry occurs. You can look for all the data you need. You can watch motion pictures, and, surprisingly, read books from one young lady to another."

"What is young lady to young lady?" My psyche was unfilled.

"That is the very thing that I came here to make sense of," she said enthusiastically.

"I haven't gotten done with showing him the rudiments of the planet at this point," diva interfered.

simon sent her away with a roll of eyes. "We'll get to that part later." simon squeezed the screen and showed me an image of two figures, standing next to each other. "Take a gander at musi ," she said. "This delightful and brilliant animal is a lady." She highlighted a figure with longer hair. "Do you see these bends? Those insane individuals? Flawlessness at its ideal."

"What is the other?" I inquired.

"Goodness that? He is a man. You don't need to stress over them. We are lesbians."

"Show him accurately," diva cautioned.

simon needed to dissent however got an opposing look from diva . "That is the very thing that she murmured." On this planet, two species are conceived, people. To separate the species, men smell crude eggs and onions, while ladies smell blossoms and cupcakes, etc. Men have harsh hands, while ladies are delicate and delightful."

"Try not to trust her musi ," diva said, folding her legs. "Not all men are that way. rashin here and there likewise scents of blossoms. Also, he appears as though he's applying cream."

"Since rashin is a beast among them," simon said with an eye roll. "Confronting this. At any rate, on this planet, people need to play snakes and stepping stools to reproduce."

"Zeus let me know it was a sort of prepackaged game," I said. "They need to play it to increase?"

"Why obviously," simon answered truly. "That is the reason they call it exhausted games. Since what they do is exhausting."

"Try not to trust that," diva immediately said. "It's an issue of inclination."

"To proceed with my illustrations," simon expressed, no matter what his accomplice. She expanded the lady on the screen. "At the point when two ladies need to play one more game called contacting the feline of the or tasting the vulva, and favors ladies to men, people call them lesbians. There is likewise a male partner, and they are called gays. On this planet, it is viewed as an abnormality by most, however in the world where you and I came from, this is the main way forward." She siphoned her arm very high.

diva gave data while simon gazed at the screen of his tablet. "Our planet is one of the numerous planets known to mankind. Just ladies live there and we can multiply without men. You can say that we are lesbians along these lines."

"Which takes me back to my past explanation which is young lady to young lady," simon finished up.

"What's more, here I believe you're showing him something beneficial," Zeus said behind us. We went to her altogether. "Come musi , I will show you your room." She conversed with diva while I got up from the sofa. "If it's not too much trouble, prepare for supper. I'm certain musi would need to taste your brilliant food."

I followed Zeus inside the room she went to before. She shut the entryway unobtrusively. "For what reason do you move with the clamor of us than us?" I inquired.

"I'm utilized to it. I was raised that way by my moms." Zeus made a signal around the room. "Yet, we haven't arrived to talk about my past. I showed you this piece since it will be yours from here on out. balica and I shared this room when she was still there, yet since you want a spot to rest, I give it to you." Her means were lighter than the breeze when she hit the sack. "I will rest in the lounge room, on the sofa."

"We don't shave the toom?"

"No... ." She gazed at the ground. "We are not permitted. On my planet... His folded temple. "My conciliatory sentiments. I generally neglect no doubt about it." Zeus actually would not look at me. "On our planet, every one of us is bound to accompany somebody. My perfect partner is your twin sister. I'm not permitted to lie in bed with anybody other than her. I'm certain you likewise have your perfect partner. You'll make her truly miserable when you share a room with me. That is the manner by which it chips away at our planet."

"Alright, yet what's miserable?" She took a gander at me rapidly and didn't reply. I sat close to her on the bed. "What?"

"Nothing. The fact that you posed the inquiry makes me significantly shocked. I said similar words to balica when I previously showed up on this planet. Might it be said that you are certain you're not her? She inhaled profoundly. "No, don't respond to that. I'm certain you are unique. The large secret is the way you isolated from her and why you were in this case. Perhaps noting that will lead us to find her as well."

"I don't see what's miserable now," I murmured. Zeus 's eyebrows rose inquisitively. "Miserable is when Zeus discusses Cairo ."

"Is that the situation?"

"Indeed. Zeus has an alternate look on his eyes." I pressed my lips. It was a propensity I saw of diva when she was discontent with simon. "I need to assist Zeus with tracking down balica , so more troubled."

The edge of her lips rose. diva let me know it was a grin. An indication of joy that was a nice sentiment. "You are a decent young lady musi . I'm certain you'll be exceptionally useful in tracking down Cairo , however for the present, what you really want to do is pay attention to our illustrations, so when we at long last go searching for it, you'll have the option to adjust. Is this unmistakable? »

"Indeed Zeus ." Something grabbed my eye on the bedside table. "What is it?"

Zeus moved his look to where I was pointing. The unusual thoroughly search in her eyes, which I have now connected with pity, returned when she saw it. She took the article from the table and took a gander at it for quite a while prior to replying. "These are called glasses. A few people have unfortunate vision by perusing excessively or watching what they call pornography."

"Pornography?"

She gestured. "simon let me know it was a show for youngsters and a many individuals watch it here." Zeus gave me the glasses. "People utilize these glasses to see better. The one you hold has a place with balica . Despite the fact that her eyes didn't require it since she's an outsider, she actually wore it consistently. She dropped it months prior."

I cummed with the glasses. simon, diva and Zeus continued to specify balica 's vanishing. The manner in which she vanished with her closest companion suddenly. It made them generally miserable. I can't help thinking about what occurred.

"Zeus ?"

"Indeed?"

"Have I made myself like Cairo ?"

She appeared to experience difficulty relaxing. "You." Zeus moved his hand to contact my face. I fixed my look on her and paused. His touch won't ever come. She dropped her hand and took a full breath. "Indeed, you do. Yet, you are not her. You are musi ." She stood up. "At any rate, how about we go to the lounge area. I can feel diva 's cooking from here. You'll adore it."

"Pause," I expressed similarly as she was going to arrive at the entryway. "What is love?"

"You need to find out for yourself," she said. "I needed to learn it the most difficult way possible." She was out of the entryway before I could figure out her response.

In the lounge area, where everybody assembled to eat, from what I found, simon and diva were at that point lounging around the table. I knew the dishes and utensils since we likewise utilized them on our movements, yet it was whenever I first tasted diva 's cooking.

"I believe you should breathe in, musi ," simon requested as Zeus assisted me with plunking down. "Do you feel that?" I gestured at him. "Recall this and recollect well. In the entire universe, just three fragrances count. The fragrance of the one you love, nature and great food like what diva served. OK? »

"Indeed simon."

"Goodness pooh-rent." She waved her hand. "Call me mother. I chose to encourage you from this point forward."

"It may not appear to be legit," Zeus commented.

"Mother," simon said on the opposite side of the table when Zeus wasn't looking.

diva reserved each privilege to be content with her cooking. The food left a wonderful desire for my mouth. It was superior to the ones individuals served during our movements. In our dinner, simon got the tablet from the table and slipped it in. She grimaced when she took a gander at the screen and quietly looked at Zeus .

"Play it," Zeus said. simon pushed on the screen and set the tablet in the table. A lady talked on screen.

"Eilmeldung," the lady said. It was in another dialect, yet my brain naturally deciphered it. "News from Briser. The Apparition Young lady, as the world knows her, was seen the previous evening at 11pm. It was followed presently by the obliteration of neighboring structures and the blast of a bomb nearby. Ten individuals were harmed and taken to emergency clinic, however the expense of the harm is considerably higher."

The view was fixated on the lady on the screen. "Who is this puzzling young lady who is by all accounts unleashing ruin from one side of the planet to the other? Is it a piece of a bigger fear based oppressor bunch? When will it be gotten? Yet, the genuine inquiry is: what does she expect of us? This is Tina from TVP, who reports."

simon took the tablet and put it on his lap. "They even called her Phantom Young lady. She's truly getting unfavorable criticism."

"Perhaps it's not exactly her," diva recommended.

simon grunted. "We both saw the CCTV film. General society has no clue about what her identity is, yet you and I know reality." She went to Zeus . "What would it be advisable for us to do as Pioneer? She's insane at this point. I realized it would happen when you didn't make the intersection. A young lady can go off the deep end on the off chance that she hasn't been sleeping for quite a while. I realize I will."

Zeus between his fingers. "We are staying on course. We have musi adjusted at the earliest opportunity, and afterward we proceed with our   quest   for   balica   ."

3

OUTSIDE

Chapter 3. OUTSIDE

A couple of days after I awakened, simon and diva felt I was all set out. They thought I had sufficient time secured in the house and was pretty much fit to be drenched in human existence. They actually haven't totally enlightened me concerning the planet we come from. However long we are on The planet, the review ought to zero in on here, they said.

"Wear your musi cap," simon requested. "The blue that Zeus gave you."

"Why?" I looked down. "Vogue says it will struggle with my outfit." I grinned at myself. I had the option to say Vogue obviously this time. A while ago when we were inside the house, simon and diva were assisting me with working on my discourse. It was practically common. Nearly. They likewise permitted me to concentrate on neighborhood magazines and mainstream societies, albeit a few things were basically lost to me.

simon halted to check my garments out. She should go to the kitchen to get her satchel. "All things considered, you know what?" She said. "Vogue lied. In this world, individuals are left and right. They say they are fine when they are plainly not. They say they read the agreements prior to tolerating anything. What's more, Vogue says the cap will make your outfit revolting when it will not. Lies, all untruths." She went on in the kitchen.

"In any case, Simon ," I moaned. It made me grin once more. Teens whimpered a great deal, the magazine said.

"I said call me mother."

I feigned exacerbation. She was Simon for me, not Mother. diva drove her head into the family room. "I discovered you feigning exacerbation," she said. "What have you been told about this?"

"Soweee," I mumbled. "Be that as it may, Simon does it a great deal. For what reason would you say you are permitted to do this and I'm not? I glared at both my sentiments and the word I said. He ought to have been grieved, not emir. I needed to make up for lost time on the off chance that I needed to play human as Zeus needed. My heart made this feeling drifting at the prospect of her. He generally did it when it came to her. I can't help thinking about why.

"Since no doubt about it," diva said. "Kids shouldn't make it happen."

"We are a similar age."

"You have a couple of days. We have been living for many years." She murmured. "I don't anticipate that you should get it, yet if it's not too much trouble, attempt to control yourself musi . Zeus would that way."

"OK."

simon returned from the kitchen. She had her satchel, as well as the cap she was alluding to. She tossed the last option at me, which I swiftly put on my head. "Our stop for now is the shopping center," she said. "This is where all people meet up to mingle and boast to one another. We should go."

We arrived at the store in a few moments. The two spoke to someone at the store while I walked around to check out the products. I saw two guys talking near the mobile section. I didn't intend to hear their conversation. "I tell you man," said the first boy. He made gestures with his fingers. "We dated, then bam! I left it for my accompaniment. Thug life baby."

The second boy hit his hand with him. "The rogue life has chosen you though."

What life were they talking about? It was nothing I read. I decided to come to them and ask them. This information could be valuable. "Uhm, excuse me."

The two turned to me. "What do you want lady? Do we have money to spend? We're just waiting for mom."

I frowned. "I realize it. But what is this rogue life that you talked about? »

"She's joking right now?" The first boy spoke. "Hey ma'am, are you kidding?"

I stood there and blinked a few times. Why would I joke about them? "No."

The second boy leaned over to his friend. "Dude, I've heard of people like her. It is… He whispered something to the other boy, which I didn't hear. They turned to me again. "How old are you, ma'am? Do you belong to a union or something like that? »

"What is it? No, I don't."

"Because we're only 9 years old, you see. But you can't intimidate us, or something like that… »

"Oh. You are older than me. I only have 27 days."
"Man, this lady is taking an additional portion of ibuprofen," says the primary kid. "I shouldn't be visible with individuals like her. We should satisfy her so she leaves." He looked towards me. "You were getting some information about the existences of hooligans?" I gestured. "OK katush," clarify it for him." He pushed the other kid before me."

katush appeared to be immediately questionable of himself prior to making sense of. "Indeed, uh. Hooligan's life is when, uh, you know, you conflict with the standard. Like when your mom says to rest at 8 a.m., yet you rest at 8:10 a.m. You are defying the guidelines. You are tight. You're loot, alright? »

"O-alright."

"Let yourself know what woman. All things considered, you seem to be a cool individual. We will give you our number and call you to show you more things. Our mom is at the checkout, so we need to go. He looked at his buddy. "Pick up the pace skion , compose your number on a piece of paper."

"I don't have a paper katush."

"You are as yet not ready." katush looked through his pockets until he tracked down a pen. He took my arm shockingly and composed numbers on my palm. "That is my telephone number, ma'am." He winked. "Try not to call after 7 a.m. I have a time limit. Also, recollect that, I want you."

"What is this dibs?"

"It resembles saying I'm the first or something to that effect," katush said. "Like the code brother. On the off chance that you want, different folks ought to ease off."

skion pushed katush once more. "That is not be guaranteed to valid," Skion said. "Regardless of whether you are the first, there is no assurance that you will remain together?"

"What do you mean?" I inquired.

"This implies that occasionally being the first isn't a confirmation that you will wrap up. It's like love. There's this young lady. The name was Felicia. She was my most memorable entirety. First young lady I permitted to sit with me on the humpback vehicle. Man, I even put something aside for our smoothie date."

"So what occurred?" Ooooh! It was energizing.

skion 's fantastic look vanished. "However at that point came Samantha." He snapped his fingers. "The young lady was great to the point that Felicia just got up and vanished from my brain. Very much like that. Thus, you see lady, since somebody has the dibs doesn't mean it's long-lasting. You can apply this with somebody you love."

Somebody I enjoyed? Like Zeus ? "Much thanks to you. I'm beginning to see now," I said.

"Great." His eyes augmented. "Good gracious, Mother is searching as far as we're concerned. Come on katush, we should push." He offered himself, yelling, "The existence of a hooligan!"

"The existence of a hooligan," katush said after him, letting me be.

simon moved toward me. She was with diva and a store staff. "Who were these kids?" simon inquired.

"skion and katush."

"Well." She went to diva . "Coincidentally, I planned to request you what tone from case you need." The store staff showed me two. One was planned with stars, while the other was strong dark. "I think dark is more exquisite," simon said. "However, which one do you like?"

I actually look at the drawings. Both were charming. Vogue said dark was as yet popular, however the cover with stars was likewise alluring. katush's voice sounded in my mind. I grinned and shrugged. "I would rather not by the same token. I will utilize the telephone without him."

The specialist laughed. I envisioned that this was what it would resemble on the off chance that she was offended as the books said. "Yet, we handpicked these drawings for you, ma'am," she said. "It's fundamentally an unfairness to utilize the telephone without inclusion. This is essentially false."

"Well," said simon. "On the off chance that musi doesn't need it, then we shouldn't compel her. How about we go compensation for things diva . Our manager provided us with huge load of cash to spend. I winked at the staff before she followed the two. The existence of Hooligan.

We left the store with paper packs close by. They got me a gadget with a name that finished with the book of words. How is it that it could be a book when it didn't seem to be a book? Odd. They likewise got me earphones for music, a tablet and a telephone. I took a psychological note to store katush's number there. Perhaps I made my new companion as the magazine said.

We then, at that point, went to a bistro. We were perched on the feathery seats when simon said, "This is the musi bistro. Where you purchase espresso and make it keep going to the extent that this would be possible." She highlighted a lady in the following table.

"See it?" simon said. "She will remain here for 4 hours. That is the means by which long espresso endures."

"Why?"

That is the means by which things are on The planet," diva said. "Furthermore, assuming you like tea, they have what you call tea sacks."

"They savor it their pack?"

"That is the thing they call the little pockets," simon made sense of. "There are a great deal of things you really want to comprehend with them. People are unique in relation to different species in the universe. Have you perused the data I advised you to peruse? »

"About our adjoining planet? Indeed Simon , I did. They are considerably more high level than people."

"That they are." She contacted her jaw. "Let yourself know what. I permit you to circumvent the shopping center for an hour and investigate all alone. It will be a decent encounter."

diva gazed at her worriedly. "Is this a smart thought? musi is only a youngster. She could get harmed."

"She will not. Furthermore, there are a ton of human gatekeepers in the shopping center. However long she doesn't leave, we will be handily cautioned if there should be an occurrence of issues. simon caused a commotion. "Do you need it?"

Good gracious! It was an open door I've generally longed for. I extolled my hands enthusiastically prior to twisting around for a fast embrace. "Much thanks to you Simon ! You are awesome! I additionally kissed diva .

"There, there," simon said with a wonderful grin. She looked at her watch. "It's the ideal opportunity for 4:30 p.m. Return at 5:30 p.m."

"I will!" I got up. "Farewell."

It was whenever I first would be distant from everyone else. I shuddered with expectation as I emerged from the bistro. With one final glance at diva and simon, I left. Oh rapture. Where might I go first? What would it be a good idea for me to see? I filtered the region until my look arrived on a huge picture on a wall. What was that? I bounced in, being mindful so as not to meet anybody in my way. Knocking was impolite, diva said. But in the room, simon said, regardless of what it implied.

I took a gander at the bright wall and heaved. There was a picture of within the shopping center. There were drawings of shops, cafés and even individuals. As an afterthought was a picture of a man. He was wearing glasses and a red and white shirt. "Where is Waldo?" I murmured to myself as I read the legend on the wall. What was that? I snapped my fingers. It resembled the analyst novel I read. Perhaps Waldo was absent in the shopping center.

I grimaced. His family members took incredible consideration to spread his vanishing. They should truly like this Waldo fellow. Perhaps I ought to attempt to help. I investigated the region. Individuals scarcely checked the wall out. People were abnormal. Waldo was missing but they would have rather not made a difference. Indeed, on the off chance that they didn't, then, at that point, I would.

A young lady came close to me and checked out at the image on the wall. "Did you track down Waldo?" She inquired.

"Have you?"

She shook her head. "No. This game is hard to play. You need to find it there." She blamed the drawing. I comprehended what she was talking about. Indeed, I probably tracked down it in the shopping center.

"All things considered, I'll go get it now," I said prior to running.

I was glancing near. There was the drive-thru eatery called Donald's or something to that effect. There were additionally shops selling garments, adornments, and so on. Alright, there was a wellspring in the center with lights of various varieties. Anything else? Where might the casualty at some point be? A drawing grabbed my eye. It was a drawing of a man in a stick with bolts pointing forward. It was only a hunch, yet consider the possibility that Waldo were there. I chose to follow the bolts. It would lead me to Waldo, very much like in wrongdoing books.

I surged my means until I saw the corner where the bolt finished. Presently I saw that there were two entryways. One with a stick-man, and one more what had all the earmarks of being a stick-woman. Waldo was a man. He could be in the entryway with the stick-man. Yet, might I at some point get in? Perhaps I ought to stroll into the other entryway and track down answers first.

With a shrug of the shoulders, I strolled into the entryway with the outline of stickwoman. It was empty. "Waldo?" I called. "Are you here?" There were different entryways, which I opened individually, just to find a latrine bowl behind it. What was this spot? It resembled a restroom yet greater. Waldo was not in any of them. I backtracked and went over somebody, a lady with long purple hair.

She took a gander at me and whistled. "balica Langley!"

"Huh? No, I'm musi . Who are you? »

She jumped. "Lies! You are balica Langley! There was a blinding flash that made me cover my eyes. When he calmed down, she was holding something bright. It looked like a weapon. "I was looking for you. mooner has been looking for you for months. Get ready to die Langley! »

She ran towards me and swung her gun. He missed me, but I hit one of the swing doors. I looked with my eyes wide open as he was cut in half. "I'm not Cairo ," I said hurriedly. She didn't listen to me as she scanned the gun again. I ran to the other side.

"Zeus is mine!" She chuckled. His face was masked with fury. "I met her first!"

"B-but I thought balica was her first."

"Lies!"

I had nowhere to run. I was trapped. With no other option, I closed my eyes. No wonder diva doesn't want me out. The world was a mess. I felt warm. Really hot. It made me open my eyes.

"Don't worry musi , I'm here," Zeus said. She ruffled my hair before holding me at full height. "I haven't seen you in months Mooner ," she told the other girl. "What are you doing?"

mooner threw her hair back behind her. "Doing the work I should have done months ago. Give me balica Langley. I looked for her."

"I looked for her too, but this girl is not balica . It's his twin sister, musi ."

"Lies!"

"Our species doesn't particularly like to lie," Zeus said. "Leave musi alone. She has no part in all this."

mooner looked in front of Zeus to look at me. I curled up behind Zeus . "She's Langley's spitting image, but you're right." She made the weapon disappear. "Its essence is different. Tsk. I thought I had it." mooner turned around. "Mark my words Zeus , I will eliminate Langley. And then I can have you." It disappeared from nothing.

Zeus waited a few seconds before looking at me. "You should be very careful musi . All right? »

My heart made this thing float again. "Yes, I am." I stared at her. She was Zeus . My Zeus . "Can I hold your hand? I'm scared." She blinked a few times and just stood there. "Please? Just once. When she didn't move, I grabbed her hand. It was warm and mild.

A thought came to my mind as I walked out of the place. That was what katush said earlier. Just because the person was the first doesn't mean they could be together. Could this also happen to balica and Zeus ? Zeus . My Zeus

4

SUBSTITUTE REALITY

Chapter 4. SUBSTITUTE REALITY

My experience in the shopping center was fleeting after we met Mooner , the purple-haired young lady. My twin sister needed to make adversaries. Basically that is everything diva said to me. I didn't actually comprehend what a foe was, however assuming there was one individual I loved the least, it was Mooner . We were returning. I was in the secondary lounge of the vehicle, attempting to have a discussion with others.

"Simon , how about you converse with me?" I inquired. She has overlooked me since Zeus took me back to them. "Are you hungry?" Hush up. Absolute quiet. simon generally had a comment. She was glancing through the window currently, viewing at the neighborhood as we passed. I tapped on diva 's shoulder. "Is there anything amiss with Simon ?"

diva met my look in the rearview reflect prior to amassing in front. She turned the vehicle to one side where our condo was and halted the vehicle. simon escaped the vehicle rapidly. Really at that time did diva at long last remove her safety belt and checked me out. "Nothing bad can really be said about her." She murmured. "simon is simply stressed over you. She was concerned in the wake of realizing what had occurred." diva connected with me and tapped my leg. "You might have been harmed."

My lips shivered. "Could it be said that she is irate with me? Was that what being crazy was like? I read it in the tattle magazine. The one where Post was the cover. Said that this young lady Taylor Shift was irate with Casey Sperry. They quit conversing with one another." I eliminated my cap. "Is that why she gives me the quiet treatment?"

A phantom of a grin played all the rage. "You rapidly take musi . However, you can definitely relax, simon isn't irate with you. She is disappointed with herself. Being on earth has instructed us that not all feelings are high contrast. Now and then it's confounded. What's more, her disappointment is there since she was the person who permitted you to walk alone in the shopping center." diva went to open her entryway. I followed her.

"I'll in any case apologize. It's my problem for being careless." I hopped inside, leaving diva by the vehicle. simon wasn't in their room when I hit. She wasn't in the kitchen or family room by the same token. She was perched on my bed and hanging tight for me. I delayed prior to joining her. "Sorry," I mumbled. "It will not reoccur, No doubt." She didn't talk. "Gracious, come on Simon , they came here for lesbian jokes."

She let out a smirk. "I'm not in that frame of mind to have one." She squeezed my cheek. "I would rather not just let it out, yet you concerned me there."

"Sorry," I said once more. Assuming there's one thing I've learned since I've been conscious, it's that individuals will more often than not say that word a great deal. They have expressed it in books, magazines and dramatizations. I changed seats, so I was confronting simon. "Do the twin sisters truly appear to be identical?"

"You can say that. Assuming they are lesbians, you can likewise tell that the twins lick each other as well."

"Huh?"

"Nothing," she says. "In any case, nod off. You are a kid. Despite the fact that you are more grounded than people, we believe you should have a completely evolved body." She was standing.

"And Zeus ? For what reason didn't she get back home with us? »

"She's continuously searching for it. Goodbye."

The dreams were strange. I've dreamed a lot since I woke up, if it even made sense. Most of them have been classified as pleasant. Sometimes I dreamed of faces I saw in magazines. The characters from the books I read would also visit me in the dream world. They would play a chapter I read from the book. The happiest dreams were for simon, diva and Zeus .

Tonight was different. I haven't dreamed of her in days. This time she had a face. She looked like me, as if I was looking in the mirror. It made me wonder if I was dreaming, or if it was real life and I was moving and breathing as if I owned his body. I followed her like a ghost. A silent spectator while I was locked in the body that was not mine.

"What do you think of rashin lie?" I asked. He sat next to me, looking at the stars. He was careful not to lean back too much, otherwise he would fall from the back of the van. Of all the vehicles we could have bought with our money, it had to be a used blue van, he complained. But I liked the truck. It reminded me of the country where I lived. Where my mother found me, thinking I was human like her. How wrong she was.

rashin turned to me. There was no comfort or assurance on his face, only worry. He was very worried these days. "Nothing," he whispered.

"I can see through you." I stuffed his ribs. "You're thinking about this girl, aren't you?"

He sighed. "You got me." rashin stared at the stars again before staring at me. "balica , why can't we just go back? Why are we doing this? »

I fought the urge to look up at him. This conversation again. He wanted to go home, which he couldn't do. I would not allow him to do that. "Because we have a goal. Everyone has a purpose. Mine remains on earth to rule this planet and humans. That's why I was sent here," I insisted. "Because humans are weak. They kill each other. They need someone like me to govern them. That must be the reason."

"But how do you know?" He said with doubt. "How do you know this is your mission in life." He put a hand on her chest. "And I'm a human being. If you think I'm weak, then you should have killed me a long time ago."

Now I really had to look up. "Don't be an idiot. You are not just any human. You are my rashin . If my mission in life is to govern humans, then yours is to help me get there. And I can't kill you. You're the only one I have."

"That's not true. You have Mrs. H. There's your sister, sia , simon, diva ." He paused. "Zeus ."

I closed my eyes to prevent it from shining. "Don't mention his name," I said between gritted teeth. "Not yet anyway." A wave of nostalgia passed through my body. I missed her too much that it became physically painful. The thought of her killed me every time. I felt like I was rotting every second I was away from her. I breathed deeply. But if I needed to endure, then I have to endure. In the end, all of this had to keep us united.

rashin 's eyes were filled with an extra dose of worry when I opened mine. "Let's go home," he begged.

"We can't. We must finish what we started. That's the only way." I put my hands on her cheeks. "You're doing this because you're curious about Mooner ."

He avoided my gaze. "There's something about her that I can't shake. It's like my soul is calling him." I chewed my lower lip. It was a very human gesture that I know, but it was a habit I got into being raised on this planet. What rashin was probably feeling was infatuation. mooner came from my planet. She had a soul mate. rashin wasn't that. As I said, the craze.

I didn't remove my hand from his face. "Remind me again who you love the most," I told him. "I thought we were in this situation together?"

"We are," he whispered.

"So stop thinking about others and straighten your head." I almost sniffed at the sentence. If simon were with us, she would joke that rashin couldn't think straight because he was like a lesbian anyway. For the second time today, I missed my friends. Shrug your shoulders from Cairo . There was no room for weakness in your heart. Not when the mission was so important. We had a goal. They would understand sooner or later. And then Zeus had no choice but to stay.

"Are you still ready to do this with me?" I asked rashin . "Because you can go home if you don't want to. But I can't come with you." I hated using the guilt card on him. He was tearing up his good heart. Still, that was the only way to keep him next to me. Somehow, I still needed rashin to stop me from doing worse things to humans.

It has expired. "You know I won't leave your side."

"Good."

A crunch on the gravel told me that our companion had returned. I stared at nash who approached us with a smile. "Sorry to cut short your lovebird conversation," she said when she was near the truck. "Did I surprise you?"

"I heard you from a mile away," I said. "And rashin is not my soul mate, Zeus is." I jumped out of the truck. "What is the status?"

nash went into report mode. I looked at her with satisfaction as she told us that the place was empty, except for the guards who wandered at night. She also modified the cameras, so that we could walk freely without being invaded by security. nash was one of my former classmates. When we were in school, I had no idea that I was an alien because I was raised on earth. She forgot she was one because of a side effect of being on this planet.

To cut it short, I later knew I was an alien, while she remembered that she was one too. When I decided to start my mission to rule the Earth, nash was the first person I contacted. She was a scientist on our planet. She was good at building things. I needed her for that.

"Tell me," I said, leaning on the truck. "Why do you really agree on this? Weren't you friends with Zeus and the others too? They would be bitterly disappointed if they realized that you work for us."

His reaction was nothing more than a shrug of the shoulders. "I'm a scientist," she said. "I like to discover things. What you arc doing right now is very interesting to me. I'd like to see how it goes."

"What about your conscience?" I said so. "So far, we have destroyed some monuments around the world." Landmarks that we could always rebuild, I remembered. "And some people were injured. Don't you think what you and I are doing is wrong? »

"There's nothing wrong when it comes to science, only facts and results. Anyway, my data confirms that the stone we were looking for is around the area. We just have to look deeper."

"How about the other? The alien we were looking for." rashin tilted his head towards the direction of our mission. "Is she there too?"

nash looked very happy with herself as she nodded at us. "Affirmative. The stone and the alien are both in the area." She made a sweeping motion with her arms. "Are we going?"

The three of us entered the place as if it was not restricted at night. We walked with confidence without worrying about video surveillance. If guards came running on us, I could easily stop them. Killing was another thing. It wouldn't be nice to get my hands dirty. But if it got to that point, I would have no choice. Sometimes you had to kill a few to save millions. In this case, billions of people on Earth. I pushed the guilt out of my heart and locked it somewhere where I couldn't feel it.

The road was illuminated by lamps on each side. There were trees and buildings. I've never been here before. It was a place of attraction. Humans would go here during the day to have fun with their families. There were sights and lots of things to explore. I wasn't there for all that. The three of us followed the road until it split in two.

Let's separate," I said to nash . "You go with rashin to the left and you look for the stone while I go the other way to look for the alien."

"Why can't I go with you?" rashin complained. "We always go together."

nash grabbed his arm and dragged him away from me. "Stop being clingy and follow me," she said. "balica can take care of herself." I said goodbye to them when rashin turned around to look at me.

"Well," I whispered to myself. "I have to look for the alien. Now, where could it be? I followed the second route. As I was looking for a possible place to find our alien, I saw one or two vehicles passing by. He was carrying two security points, patrolling the place. Each time, I dodge to the side to avoid confrontations. It was for them, not mine.

It didn't take me long before I came across a small, house-sized building. It didn't seem like it was one of the main attractions of the place. It must have been where some of the employees lived. I broadened my senses. It was a good benefit that came with being an alien, and I've been using it for months now. My senses told me that the building was currently occupied by one person. And she wasn't human. Bingo!

I was right to think that the building was not an attraction but a place for employees. There was a living room I was walking through, and a cozy kitchen full of appliances. Most of the rooms had five bunk beds. I found my alien sitting on one. Like any other species that came to Earth, she was beautiful. She wore her short black hair. Trimmed on the sides, smoothed backwards in the middle. She was sturdy, although her soft face and dark brown eyes told me she was very feminine.

Leaning near the door frame, I asked, "What is your name?"

She looks away from her phone to check on me. Her expression said she knew what I was, and I knew what she was. Touchdown. She placed the phone on the bed. "You are the guest. You have to tell me your name first."

"What if you were a gracious host and answered the question?"

She stood without answering me. "If you want to kill me, then I suggest you do it first." His eyes were shining. "Keep going. Use your hands, grab your neck and kill yourself."

I laughed at him. "If we were in school, it would be classified as bullying." She frowned. I kept going. "Anyway, I heard about your power. You have the ability to suggest." I stretched my arm. "I'm not here to kill you. I'm here to recruit."

"Kill yourself," she repeated in a more murderous tone.

"As I said. I know your power." Thanks to nash 's sources. "I also know he has limits. For example, you can only use the suggestion if the person is emotionally distraught or physically disabled. A person who drank alcohol for example." I sneered. "My friend simon always told me that I am a boring person. I don't drink, so good luck with that." I shrugged my shoulders. "Outside of this power, you are just as weak as humans."

She matched my sneer. "While you may not be intoxicated, no one is completely emotionally stable." She took a step towards me. "Everyone has something that concerns them. Anger. Feared." She leaned into my ears and whispered. "At someone's request. Someone you love."

My thoughts went astray to Zeus . It made me motionless. The pain of being away from her also whipped my body. Has she experienced this as well? Did I miss Zeus so much?

The alien laughs loudly. "I may be as weak as a human, but I can easily kill you like that. Don't move." This time, his power of suggestion wrapped up in my body. It was like invisible ropes, preventing me from moving as she said. The alien easily placed his fingers around my neck and squeezed. I was choking. Gradually, life was exhausted from me.

"Oh no, you won't!" rashin screamed as he attacked the alien. It freed me in an instant.

"How did it go. You. You know? I said between short breaths. "That I was in trouble?"

nash walked into the room. "We were near this place when rashin ran, saying he could feel you." She shook her head with amusement. "You're so clingy that sometimes I wonder what's going on."

"Nothing happens," I gasped. rashin subdued the alien.

"Anyway," nash tells the alien. "We are here to recruit you as we have done with others. balica has a purpose, and either you are with her or against her. I know for a fact that aliens do not usually come to Earth by their free will. You must have done something on your planet that made you hide here."

The alien pulled rashin 's hand from him. She reluctantly massaged her wrist. "Hmph! What do you know? »

"I know a lot," nash says.

My lung cleared. I was able to breathe well. "What do you call yourself extraterrestrial?" I told the girl. "Don't make me repeat."

She met my gaze. "marlina . You can call me marl."

I reached out to shake his hand. It was cold and sweaty. She didn't trust me yet. OK. Never trust me. "Welcome to the marlina Group. I am   balica   ."

5

STEALTH VISION

Chapter 5. STEALTH VISION

The dream I had last night was so real. Even though I sat in bed awake the next morning, I felt a sense of confusion, wondering if I was musi or Cairo . I dreamed of her again. My so-called twin. The one Zeus and the others were looking for. Without wasting another second, I went to the kitchen and told Simon about it.

"Describe it to me again musi ," Zeus said. I was lucky that she was still at home when I told my dream. She usually left earlier.

"In my dream," I say automatically. "balica was with a male specimen she called rashin , and a girl named nash ."

Simon slammed his fist on the table. It wasn't that difficult, but it was enough to spill his bottled water. "I knew it!" She said. "I knew she had gone with balica ."

"Who?" I asked simon.

"nash ." She frowned. "nash is an alien like us. She is a scientist. Months ago, when balica disappeared, nash disappeared without a trace. We were worried about her, but we didn't know where to look. I suggested that she could have joined balica and rashin ." She turned to diva with a smile. "See? I won our bet. I will melt you so hard. »

"What is it?" I asked before diva could say anything.

"Something you don't need to know until you're a thousand years old," Zeus said. "Pursue your dream and ignore simon."

"She'll know eventually," simon actually said. "And she'll love it."

Ignoring him as Zeus instructed him, I immersed myself in the tale. "So balica , rashin and nash talked to another girl and befriended her. Then they went together to a huge castle. There are statues of people with pointed hats. Oh and chopsticks." I frowned as I tried to remember. "I think there's also a broom handle."

simon was selfless. "Maybe it's just a weird dream. It seems far-fetched to me."

Zeus raised his hand to silence simon. "It's possible. But you've forgotten that musi has never seen photos of rashin and nash before, and her description of how they look is strange. If she was able to tell what they look like, then the dream must be related to real life. Let's see why she was able to see it later, after we went to that place."

"But where can you find a castle with brooms, people with pointed hats and chopsticks?" diva asked. "You think they have that in Germany?"

"I know where it is, and it's not in Germany." The four of us turned to the doorway. A little girl with a pink rabbit headband came in with a huge smile on her face. "Hi Aunt balica ," she said casually. "How did it go?"

"Who are you?" I said so.

"Let's talk outside of sia ," Zeus said almost at the same time.

The child looked at me at questioning Zeus , shrugged his shoulders, and then went to the door with Zeus . simon and diva were all over me when they left.

"Remember what we told you about adopting Cairo on earth?" diva said. I nodded. They explained to me earlier that balica was raised by a woman they called Mother in the Country. "Well, this kid is balica 's niece," diva continued. "She doesn't know her aunt is an alien, and what's more, she has no idea that balica is missing."

I frowned. "How could you keep the information for him for months?"

"Lies," simon simply said. "I told you about this thing called lying, didn't I? People do it all the time on this planet. All we had to do was lie to her about how busy balica was studying for this great semester, so she could get to a good college. Worked like a charm. The only problem is that sia can't stay away from her aunt long enough, and now she's here visiting."

"But isn't lying bad? I saw it in the afternoon drama. This Mars girl was so hurt when someone lied to her."

simon shrugged. "Think of it as a meticulous assembly. Good writers do it."

I nodded. It made sense. Simon was the expert. I should listen to him. "What should I do?"

His eyes shone mischievously. "Are we proud."

Zeus and sia returned to the kitchen after a few minutes. They smiled at each other as if they were having a good conversation. They stopped in front of me. "Pante balica ," sia said seriously. "Zeus told me you were sick."

"I am?"

simon put his arms around me. "Of course you are. You have what we call licktomania. It's the desire to include girls in your meal plan."

"simon," Zeus warns. "We have two children in the house."

"I'm no longer a child," sia and I said at the same time.

"You both are," Zeus says. "Back to our initial conversation before simon intervened. I told sia about your recent illness. On how you forgot some things and are trying to recover your memory." Zeus knelt before sia so that they were at eye level. "You won't tell Mother, will you? I will give you sweets and ponies."

"ray lovig?" sia asked, I hope.

"Yes, I will give you this animal, as long as you do not tell Mother what is happening. She will worry about Cairo . And if you can, call her musi for now."

"Why?"

"Because that's what we want to call it."

"Of course. You can count on me Zeus ." sia glanced at me. "And you too Aunt musi ." I breathed a sigh of relief. At least she didn't want to confuse me with my twin, although technically she didn't understand anything. Zeus helped sia sit on the counter by lifting her up. They were cute together. Do Zeus and I also look good together?

"As I said earlier, I know where you can find a castle, a wand, pointed hats, and things like that." sia was excited as she said, "Universal Studios."

With diva 's fast driving, we arrived on site shortly. After buying what they called tickets, which I found to be a piece of paper that you would have to give to people on admission, we were finally let in. Note to yourself. Humans liked to collect small things like handkerchiefs, bills, etc. I should ask Zeus and others later why they did it.

"Is this the place of your dream?" simon said.

I took a look around the area. No doubt about it. balica and her friends came here. The entrance was the same. The same was true for roads and signs. Except now there were a large number of people walking and talking to each other. There were also long queues. "That's it," I told them. "They first went to a smaller building before heading to the castle."

"In the dream," says Zeus . "Was there anything they were doing in particular?"

"They befriended a girl named marlir. Then they looked for a stone."
sia , who was barely paying attention when we arrived, was now looking at us with a puzzled expression on her face. "Who are you talking about?" She asked. "Why did we go here in the first place?" The child insisted on coming with us. Now she was asking questions that I didn't know how to answer.

diva was quick to say, "We went to this place because rashin found a job here. We will pick it up and have fun. Yes! »

"That's right," Zeus said with equal expression. During the days I got to know her, I observed that compared to simon, diva and sia , her expression was always the same. It's rare that she changes it, unless we're talking about Cairo . It made me curious about their relationship. Was that what love was? My stomach turned. I had a funny feeling when I thought of them together.

"It would be easier if we separated." Zeus reported to simon and diva . "Take sia with you. Find the building musi described."

"What about me?" I said so.

"You come with me. We will check the castle."

Zeus and I took a bus. We sat side by side silently in the middle part. As the bus went along, someone spoke to all of us in front. She said she was a tour guide. The seat was big enough for Zeus and me, but somehow I could feel it smaller over time. Imadivation, the books said. It was a comfortable trip with her next to me. She always gave me a pleasant feeling.

I checked the guide opposite. She said something about movies and effects. I decided to listen to it later. This was my chance to talk to Zeus . It wasn't every day that we were left alone like this without simon and diva . I smiled at myself. Maybe I could find something new about him.

"What are you doing on our planet?"

She stared at me. "Why did you ask?"

"Because you know me, but I don't know about you. In the books I've read, when two people meet, they usually tell each other something about each other. It just seems like you're giving me some information about yourself."

She continued to look at me with the same illegible expression. Zeus was sitting by the window, and although sunlight played with her hair and face, it wasn't my Maldive tion when her eyes briefly changed to an orange color. It was by the way because it changed right away. To this day, the look knew me well. She didn't try to hide it in the house. Outside, I knew she had to be careful not to scare humans. No other being in the universe had orange eyes except her.

"In your lessons with diva and simon, did they tell you about leadership roles on earth?"

I remembered the presidents and all that. "Yes," I replied.

She changed so she could look at me from a better angle. "On our planet, the ranking is as follows. There is the normal citizen. It is the workers. They do great things to make our lives better. Then there are the guards. There are two groups of guards, one for citizens and the other for royalty."

Royalty? Like a king? »

"You can say that. Anyway, after the citizen and the guards, there is the council. They are voted by citizens to establish and enforce laws. But you know what's even better? I shook my head and his face lightened a little. "Royalty has the last word. They can easily change the laws."

"Anytime?"

"At any moment," she replied. "Of course, the new law should still benefit citizens because our planet operates on a symbiotic ecosystem. Always remember that. Each action triggers something else musi . Nothing is a coincidence when it comes to our species." I took the information like a sponge. It was really the first time I heard more on our planet. simon and diva 's teachings were centered on the earth. They said that our lessons about our planet connected to Zeus .

"Tell me more," I said. "What happens after the council?"

"There's royalty of course. But we also have a ranking on this. The Queen takes the highest seat. She is the sovereign and can live for many millennia. They said that our first Queen was born when the universe was created. Our species are old."

"Is the Queen dying?"

I felt a change in his mood. It wasn't obvious on his face. But her aura suggested that she was bothered by something. "Unfortunately, everything in the universe ends up ending," she explained. "In time, the Queen will join our ancestors, a dust in the flow of life. We are now in the third cycle of Queens."

"Tell me about our queen," I said with good interest. "Is she beautiful? Powerful? What does it look like? »

Zeus 's illegible mask flickered. For a second, I saw worry on his face. It disappeared just as quickly. "The current queen is a selfish leader. A kid. She cares too little about her own species and cares about no one but herself." She relaxed on her seat. "But for all her flaws, the queen has a trait that everyone can be proud of. She loves deeply and truly."

"Oh… How can you say that? »

The color of his eyes became entirely orange. "Because she escaped her guards and left her own planet after being crowned in search of her wife."

"B-but." I gasped. "That means you are…"

She glanced out the window. "Yes. balica doesn't know yet. I didn't tell her because I wanted her to be comfortable with the idea of her true nature first. But time is of the essence. There is a few months of gap between our planet and Earth when you travel using the wormhole. To date, the returning guards have had to take several ships to pick me up. diva and simon should have stayed there to control the situation. They were my second in command. »

"They are also royalty."

"Yes. We grew up knowing our place on the planet and in the universe."

"But if balica is your wife, then why is she on earth? Why am I? »
    She shook her head. "My intention is to answer the same question myself before I go home. But before we can do all this, we must first get Cairo back. There is no other way." The bus stopped. People began to get up from their seats, standing in the middle aisle to get out of the vehicle. The tour had to end without us noticing.

"There is our destination," Zeus said as he pointed to the castle outside. "Let's go."

I pounded behind her and the other passengers. A large castle stood on us. "Look, there is a dragon statue on a stone building." I turned to another corner. "There is a weird alley on this road." I went around. "There are so many people. Wow! Humans, I want to pinch them all. It's like the mall, only better." I glanced at Zeus . "Aren't you impressed?"

"There is also a dragon on our planet. A real one and not made of stone. diva has the power to control it, including any animal." She started walking towards the alley.

"What about simon?"

"It is connected to nature."

I walked in front of her and made a pivot, so I walked back looking at her. It was a good way to continue the conversation. So I could see his face comforting. "What about you?"

"As I said, the Queen is selfish. Now walk properly or you could hurt yourself musi ." I turned around with a scowl. All three treated me like a child. It is true that I was a few days old and was nowhere near their age. However, my body looked like theirs. They feed me too much.

We continued down the alley. The farther we went, the fewer people we met. We walked until Zeus paused near a wall. She squatted on the ground. "What are you doing?" I asked as she swept her finger on the floor.

She snorted her hand. "I can feel the traces of a mineral. I don't know what it is."

"Let's go around the place. Maybe we can find the main source of mineral somewhere." I felt disappointed when I realized that I had mispronounced the word again.

Zeus noticed my squeaky face and stood up. "You will get used to speaking this language. Don't worry so much about that of our planet. It's easier to learn because you're a child who hasn't been taught much about the universe. Although I doubt balica will find it that easy."

"Do you miss her? balica , I mean. You get into the habit of comparing me to her. Do you have trouble looking at me? I was a child to them, but I knew how to think. I could put two and two together.

Her eyes narrow before she glances at the floor. "I don't miss her. I'm completely broken." She sighed. "It makes me crack when I think about it because our species would have forgotten how to use our emotions, but here I am, feeling everything at once."

I was in front of her in a few steps. My heart was pumping twice as fast. She smelled good. Like the sun and flowers. "So, please, look at me more. I wouldn't mind if you claimed I'm her." My hand was shaking as I reached out to tilt his face towards me. "We all live in the same house, and you all found me together. But somehow, you are different from simon and diva . I wonder why this is the case."

"Stop," she whispered, closing her eyes. The orange threatened to come out again.

"Stop what? I don't do anything."

His eyes opened. "Just stop."

I dropped my hand. "As you wish."

simon suddenly materialized next to us. It shocked me to see her like that. She came out of nowhere. "Leader," she said. "diva spotted balica a few seconds ago. Let's go." Zeus and simon did not linger. Both disappeared, leaving me alone, not knowing what my place on earth   was.   In   the   universe.   With   Zeus   .

6

MEETINGS

Chapter 6. MEETINGS

zeus and Simon left for a total of ten minutes. There was no sign of them or if they would come back to pick me up. Life in the theme park went on as I stood in the same place without moving. People who passed by were more captivated by their friends or where they should go next. It was even though I was non-existent.

I decided to explore on my own. zeus and simon would be busy for a while, I thought. Maybe I'd find what or who they were looking for if I walked too. I kept my eyes open all the time to observe humans. Rarely were they seen alone. They have always been with a large group of people. If I came across a single person, they would avoid eye contact or take out their phone to look at it even if they didn't do anything. What for?

Above the sound of the human's chatter, two voices stood above everything. "I want to go to the henchmen skion ."

"I vote for the katush Mummies. The henchmen are overrated anyway."

I smiled at myself as I recognized the voices. katush and skion , the two kids I met at the mall. They were in the middle of an argument when I went to see them. Dark hair, small and skinny. They stopped and stared as I approached. The way they sewed each other, they recognized me too.

"Oh look, there's bae," katush said. He was the smallest boy among the two.

"Baby?" I asked. "Isn't it Danish for poop?" My wide vocabulary also allowed me to move from English to other languages. Benefits of being an alien, simon said.

skion scratched his head. "What century are you of Lady? Bae means that I make you heart. Like boyfriend and girlfriend stuff." He crossed his arms confidently. "Like when you say, hey, come down for a little something?"

I frowned. "What is something? And why do you talk like that? They looked different from what I was used to. "Is it related to the life of a thug that you used to say?" I remembered that they were shouting the word rogue life in the store.

skion laughed. "No family. That was the past. We are well above that now. Isn't it katush ? »

katush nodded seriously. "Yes, we are." He stared at me curiously. "Why are you here? Do you follow us? »

"No. I went here with my friends. We separated to look for something, and then my partner left me looking for a girl."

katush and skion settled significantly. "You have been dropped." skion explained it to me well. "See when someone leaves you for someone else, you're not the top priority. This is not good. You should know your lady who is worth it."
   "I'm not sure I understand."

katush tilted his head. "Come with us."

I found out that katush and skion came here with their parents. They were currently playing hide and seek with mom and dad. Their parents were so cool to play this game with them in the big theme park. The boys and I walked while talking. It was as if the people around us were the props of a film set. We barely noticed them.

"Spill the beans," skion says.

"Spoiling food is bad."

He sighed. "I wanted to tell us everything. You're on crack again." I didn't ask what crack meant.

"Okay." I breathed before I said, "I like this person a little bit, but this person has a girlfriend."

"Where is the girlfriend?" skion asked.

"I don't know. She ran away." I shrugged my shoulders. "Anyway, I love this person more and more and I don't know what to do."

skion touched his chin thoughtfully. "Is it a normal like, or a like-like? Because there is a difference. When it's normal, you can easily forget about that person. He says it in the movie I watched. But," he stressed. "If it's a similar one, you have a problem. It's harder to forget the family."

katush grabbed my hand. His was very small. "But then you will be a homewrecker. Because the person has a girlfriend. And it's not good."

I nodded at them. "I see… Maybe I'll forget my like for her."

katush let go of his hand and stared at me curiously. "Lady, are you gay?"

"I guess. My friends told me I was, but I'm not sure."

skion pointed the finger at a guy in the distance. "Do you see this guy? Does it wet your diapers? Mom used to say that if you're a gay girl, boys won't do anything about your diapers. She said that because my sister is gay."

I checked the type. He was tall. Broad shoulders. It looks like he was looking for someone, but I couldn't quite see his face because it was clogged with his cap. I shook my head. "No… He doesn't."

"You're definitely gay," katush said. "What type are you? There are a lot of them according to my sister." He rubbed his hands together. "There's the woman, the lipstick, the power dam, the sports dam, just the dike, the baby dam, the butch, the lesbian, the Gayle , the lesbian lonestar, the lesbian gold star and the queen of the pillow." He inhaled deeply, looking like he had run the marathon. "Phew! That's a lot. What do you identify with? »

"I don't know," I admitted. It was difficult to take everything at once. I promised to do some research on this later.

"Anyway," Skion said. "The fact is that if you love this person, just know that there will be consequences. She took the man. The girlfriend may get angry."

"You're there. I looked for you everywhere." A hand rested on my shoulder. I turned around to see the guy of my dreams last night. "I thought you were walking around the park, but it took you over five hours. I had to spend the night sleeping in the truck." He noticed that skion and katush were standing next to me. "And according to her appearance, you even made balica friends."

"I'm not Cairo ."

"Of course you are." He placed an arm around me. "Say goodbye to your new friends because we are leaving." rashin took off his hat, nodded to the children, and then dragged me along. I looked at him helplessly. The others were looking for his group. If he was here, Cairo was still there too. I need to contact zeus . Sliding my hand into my pocket, I took out my new mobile phone.

Take a look and rashin grabbed the phone for me. He dropped it to the ground to my surprise and broke it with his boots. My eyes watered. simon and diva gave it to me. "You're bad!" I screamed. "It was a gift." I got on my knees to pick up the pieces. Simon would be so crazy.

rashin was also on his knees, helping me with a disoriented look on his face. "I thought we weren't going to use it anymore? You said there was no connection to our family, did you? It was you who taught that Cairo ."

I made fun of him. "I'm not Cairo . My name is musi ."

He stopped moving. rashin stared at me, and I really wanted to look at myself this time. The realization appeared on his face. "Oh my God," he whispered. "Who are you?"

I stood up, the pieces broken in my hands. "I've already told you my name." I wiped away tears angrily. He was such a nice boy in my dreams. No! He destroyed my phone. "You will buy me a new phone. Before simon and diva find out."

He still couldn't recover from my face. rashin avala. "O-okay."

rashin and I sat silently in the taxi. I refused to talk to him when he was just staring at me all the time. He couldn't stand it anymore. He finally said, "I've known balica and her family for years. I have never seen you once. Where are you from? »

The capsule and the island came to mind. I doubt zeus and the others would appreciate him if I told him. And I really didn't want to discuss it right now. "I don't say it until you get me a phone," I say stubbornly.

Stop," he told the taxi driver.

Five minutes later, I had the exact phone model safely stored in my pocket. I wanted to call the others, but I was afraid that rashin would destroy him again. We walked down the side street to look for a taxi for our return trip. "Hey." He took my arm gently. "I got you the phone. Tell me about yourself."

I tore off my arm. "I am balica 's twin sister."

"Are you also an alien?"

"Shhhhh!"

He looked foolishly around. "Sorry. I always forget." He pressed his hand on the pocket of his jeans. rashin was bigger than I remembered in my dream. "Then," he said awkwardly. "Where did you live before that? And I think you mentioned Simon and diva 's name. How well do you know them? »

"Good enough to know that they are looking for you and my sister." It was my turn to grab his arm. "Come with me. I'll show it to them."

"I can't. We have a mission to accomplish first. He blinked. "Gosh, you really look like him. I never knew she had a twin. It's like I'm dreaming." I pinched his arm hard. "Oh! What did I do?"

I walked in front of him, my hands on my back. "Now you know that you are awake." I smiled as he followed with a frown. He did not come back. rashin was a kind soul after all. We decided to walk to the theme park. It was pretty close anyway. We just entered the premises when rashin pulled me to the side, where a large group of people were huddled. "What are we doing?"

He put a finger on his lips, telling me to shut up. rashin glanced behind the group of people and relaxed. "Nothing. A friend of mine named nash passed by. I don't think she should see you."

"Why?"

"Because she would talk about you in Cairo , and I don't want balica to be more confused than she is right now." He took off his cap. "Frankly, I just want to go home, but it's not in the plan yet."

"What's not in the plan?"

rashin groans when he sees another girl approaching. "I thought I told you to stay in the car?" He said.

The girl stopped in front of me. His face jumped out of my dream. Was marlina ? Robustness and femininity in one package. I reached out to introduce myself. "Hi, I'm musi . Nice to meet you."

marlina was about to touch my hand when rashin stopped it. "balica has a twin," he quickly said. "What she doesn't know. If it happens between the two of us, I don't know what I'm going to do with you."

"Are you threatening me?" marlina asked.

"I've never been one to threaten." His jaw muscle trembled. "But when it comes to Cairo and protecting her best interest, I'll be ready to do anything. Even if you are an alien." They looked at each other head down before marlina

shrugged.

"That's your problem to solve, I guess," she said. "I'm just here for the ride." marlina turned to me with a smile and offered his hand. "You can call me marl ."

"Hello," I said politely.

She didn't just hold hands. She meandered her arms around my waist and whispered. "Where have you been all my darling life?" rashin asked me marl with a scowl. "Hey," she complained. rashin walked between us.

"I don't like to see that," he said. "It's like you're touching balica ."

"What is the evil?" marl said. "I am a girl."

"Who loves girls," rashin provided. "And as far as I'm concerned, balica belongs to zeus . I will only abandon it for one person."

marl pushed rashin in a playful way. They met last night according to my dreams. They were like good friends now. "Save Romeo. This girl is not balica . You said it yourself, didn't you? She is a twin. You can do the movements now."

rashin fully realized that she was right. "Again," he said. "You have to respect her as if she were Cairo . And besides, I have known you for a few hours to understand that you are a killer. IIc's not the best person to hang out with."

"Do you also like girls?" marlin told me cheerfully. "Because your sister does."

"We came from the same planet." That should explain everything.

rashin remembered something. "Where is zeus ? Why were you alone when I found you? He inquired.

"They went to get balica . Why won't she go home? This was not my own question, but something that zeus and the others had been thinking about for months.

"Because she's a fool," marlina said. "World domination? Ha! Don't make me laugh." She put her hand in her pocket, only to reveal a pack of cigarettes. rashin snatched it and threw it away long and hard. I didn't see where he landed. marl didn't look interested, as if it were nothing new. "Guess that old habits die hard."

"I told you not to smoke in front of me," rashin said to justify his actions.

marl smiled. "You're a big guy, but you harass yourself like a woman." She grabbed his chest and squeezed. "Pities". She looked disappointed as she let go of her hand. "I thought for a while that you were one. Wouldn't it be easier that way? Both for you and for this mooner girl."

rashin 's jaw clenched. "I never said I loved him."

"That's why your eyes were shining brightly when nash told me about aliens on earth so far," she laughed. "Who are you kidding? You love it as much as you did with balica . Who is the killer now? »

rashin was about to answer when his head went up. "Cairo ," he says. "Something happened to him. I can feel it." He bolted himself without saying goodbye.

marlina 's face was full of regrets when she glanced at me. "Guess I have to catch up with you later. She kissed my hand. "We see ourselves beautiful."

I have several questions in mind. Why did he feel like everyone was leaving me alone for Cairo ? Was his existence more important than mine? Why did everyone love him? And more importantly, I thought as I walked away in the other direction. Why did I know rashin was right when he said something was happening to Cairo ? Because the moment he said those words, I felt a tightening in my heart as if I was   dying.

7

GUESS

Chapter 7. GUESS

Eventually, the other aliens came back to me. They didn't look very happy. zeus in particular didn't want to talk. simon told me to leave the subject alone as we drove to the car. But I heard her speak in a low voice to her partner, saying that zeus had met balica in the theme park. If balica wasn't with us, then zeus couldn't bring her back.

After thinking about it a few times, I concluded that balica was a valued member of their group. That everyone wanted his presence. But why? She was no prettier than me. We shared the same face. Maybe it was the time spent with her. Perhaps they had experiences that all species enjoyed. Maybe, maybe, maybe. There may be. The answer escaped my brain which barely understood the concept of things.

A week after this incident, Simon, diva and I were found chatting in the kitchen. It was after breakfast. zeus didn't join us anymore. She has been sticking to herself since returning home. She didn't talk much and didn't leave her room when it wasn't time to eat. Simon and diva were convinced that something was wrong, and that was the topic of our conversation.

"This has never happened before," simon said. "Our boss barely talks to us. It seems that she does not see us. I don't think she's taking a shower either. She wore the same thing twice this week." Simon took the fork from his plate and tried to balance it so that it stood on the table.

"I'm sure she took a shower," I said. My face turned warm. "I picked up his dirty clothes to wash them."

"Yes," diva agreed. "And our boss owns three of those shirts. You gave it to his last Christmas, didn't you? »

The fork fell on the table with a clang. "Now that you mention it, I gave him a lot of identical clothes," simon said as he picked up the fork again. "But that's irrelevant. zeus always acts in strange ways. I don't like it. She's not like that."

diva got up and started picking up the dirty plates from the table. She tore simon off the fork before going to the sink. I heard his voice above the flowing water saying, "Do you think our leader finds anything?"

"I don't think so, I know it," simon said confidently. "We have been on this planet for too many months. Perhaps she contracted a disease unique to our species. I mean, you became more emotional than usual diva , and I got Satan's stunt. I think the leader is also experiencing something."

I blinked a few times at Simon. "What is Satan's waterfall? And what is a Satan? »

Simon smiled at me. "You have a lot to learn about the young human. Satan is a fictional character created by people. Sometimes he disguises himself as blood from the hole. Don't ask me what hole it is. Determine it. And sometimes he disguises himself as a purple dinosaur named Barney to scare the kids at night." Simon's smile turned into an evil smile. I shuddered.

diva laughed as she washed the dishes. "Don't teach musi these things." She looked at me over her shoulder. "Humans believe that this character of Satan takes the form of many things. Sometimes a beautiful woman to seduce people. He also invents lies to achieve his ends."

"Like Simon?" I asked.

"Not exactly. Simon is not bad. Satan is."

"That wasn't what you said last night," simon said. "I remember you called me a bad girl."

diva 's face blushed. She quickly turned her head away, returned to her dishes. "We are deviating from the subject here. If you are convinced that our leader is finding a disease, what should we do? »

simon pushed back his chair to stand. She positioned her leg on the chair and raised a finger to the ceiling, as if she had a brilliant idea. The magazine called people like her theater. "We need to find a cure before it gets worse," she said. "diva , you're coming with me. We leave at dawn."

"It's 7 a.m.," I whispered. "We just had our breakfast."

"We then leave after washing the dishes. musi , you stay here and you keep the house."

The two left me after doing the dishes and taking a quick shower. They said it was an important operation to save the leader, and I, being the youngest, should stay in place until further notice. Having nothing better to do, I paced the living room while glancing at zeus 's door from time to time. I did it until I got tired. If something was wrong with her, I should know once and for all. simon and diva shouldn't be the only ones with this responsibility.

I knocked on the door with hesitation. "zeus ? It's me, musi . Does it bother you that I open this door to talk to you? My voice was smaller than I remember, bordering on the shy side. Why did my treatment with zeus have to differ from others? Was it because she was the leader?

"Okay," said his faint voice. I opened the door and glanced. The curtains have been drawn. Only light from a small crack made by the curtains illuminated the room. It was dark even though the sun was high outside. zeus was sitting on the bed. "Can I do something for you?" She asked. His voice was the same. She had the same appearance. But there was something different about her. As if she had lost her spark.

I stayed by the door. "Do you feel good?"

"Yes." Ten seconds of silence passed. It was so quiet that I could hear the tick on my wristwatch. "Is there anything else?" She asked. My brain couldn't form anything coherent. I shook my head and muttered no.

Back at the show, I was reduced to the rhythm again. Something happened. Simon and diva were right. zeus was acting strangely. What must I do? She was not only our leader, but also someone who worried me. Maybe that's what humans called worry. I was experimenting with it, and I didn't like it.

I fished the phone out of my pocket, remembering that rashin had replaced it for me. The number I used was always the same. I checked the phone recordings. There wasn't much on the list other than the alien's numbers. I haven't had time to make more friends yet. But there were some people I could ask for help from. Who better than a human to consult on diseases since we were on earth.

I found katush 's number and called him. It took ten rings before it picked up. Somehow, I was happy to hear his voice in the other line. "Yes, it's my daughter Janna?"

"No, it's me musi ."

"Oh musi mah another woman. What's up? I could hear strange noises from the other line. Constant click noise.

"What are you doing?" I asked.

"Playing Smash Brothers with skion ."

"You mean losing to skion ," I heard the other child say. The click noise became louder.

"Oh. I didn't want to be disturbed, but I'd really like to ask for your help." I changed the phone for my other ear. "I don't have many friends yet, you see, I have days and everything. I was wondering if you would give any advice."

"What does she say?" skion asked.

"Our dawg needs advice." The click sound stopped.
    "You're so bad at this katush ," skion said. "When someone needs advice, you give them priority, especially if they're a friend." I heard a clifle followed by a scream from katush . "Homies for man

for life. Here, let me talk to him. Hello? skion 's voice became louder. He was the one holding the phone now, I guessed.

"Hey."

"Sup girl. What does it take? »

I didn't want to waste any more time, so I immersed myself in it. "Do you remember that girl I loved? I think she is sick. I want to help him but I don't know what to do. She hasn't spoken to us properly for days, and she's in her room most of the time."

"Eh oh… Girls' problems. Stay online. I know an expert." There was a crackle before he shouted, "Ashanti. Shanti, come here." A break. "Shanti," he shouted louder. "The sofa is on fire." The footsteps sounded, as if someone was running.

"There is no fire!" A girl's voice said. "I'm going to twist your ear, little punk!"

"I'm sorry! I am sorry! skion pleaded.

"Don't call me for something stupid."

"Oh!" skion screamed. "I said this because you're too busy and you wouldn't go down otherwise. I really need your help."

"Help with what?" The girl said suspiciously. skion told him about my problem. I could hear them clearly from the phone. "I think I know what this disease is," she finally said. "Tell your friend to ask the sick person if they missed their period. If the answer is yes, call me as soon as possible. It's an emergency."

"Have you heard that?" skion told me. "This is my older sister Shanti. She's an expert."

An unpleasant sensation was in my stomach. An emergency was bad, wasn't it? I was more worried about zeus than before. "Yes, I heard your sister. I will ask you right away and call you back." I turned to zeus 's gate at the end of the call. It was bad. Really bad. I didn't bother to knock before opening the door. "Did you miss your period?" I asked without saying hello.

"I don't have any rules. In a way, yes, I've been missing it for a while."

"Thank you." I closed the door and dialed my friend's number as I walked to the kitchen. skion picked up after a ring. "She missed her period," I said.

"Shanti," he shouted. "The girl missed her period."

"Oh my God!" Shanti said. His voice sounded far away. "Tell your friend to ask the sick person if they feel like anything, or to check for signs of nausea and vomiting."

"Did you hear that?" skion asked for the second time.

"As clear as I hear you now," I said. "Okay, I'll call you back right away. Thank you." I walked to zeus 's room and took a look. She was still sitting on the bed. "Do you want something?"

"Nothing in particular."

"Are you sure? You have to be, right? »

His eyebrows furrowed. I could see it even when it was dark. "Now that you've mentioned it, I haven't eaten meliod yet. I read in a book that some people like this green thing. I'm curious to know what exactly it looks like and what it tastes like. We don't have that on our planet."

"Do you say you want to?" I prayed.

"I don't have much appetite, but I guess so."

I slammed the door and took a deep breath. She was sick. My zeus was sick. simonand diva would find a cure for sure. They are getting better. I dialed skion 's number. "She wants to be a lawyer. Where can I get this? »

"On the market. Take a bus or take a ride to nice people to get there. katush and I do it all the time. You just need to point your thumbs up when a car passes. If they stop, you tell them where to go. Is it? »

"Yes." I walked quickly to the living room and grabbed my coat from the couch. simonand diva always told me not to leave the house. Not this time. It was for zeus . Maybe the lawyer would make him feel better until the other aliens arrive. Taking one last look at zeus 's door, I walked out.

The first three cars that passed didn't slow down or stop for me. It was in the fourth attempt that a red van made. The windows on the passenger side went down. A very nice lady with sunglasses said, "Where are you going for the young woman?"

"I need lawyers." I smiled at him. They were nice to stop for me.

She took off the sunglasses and hung them on her shirt. The woman's eyes were like diva 's, smaller and friendlier in one way or another. "My family and I are going to obonte . There are lawyers there. Would you like to come? »

"As long as there are lawyers."

They let me squeeze in the back. The woman was with her husband and children. I thought all six were their children, but only one of them was. The others were cousins. The husband drove strangely, as he took smaller roads instead of the main road as diva always did. It was a shortcut, the family said. Soon we arrived at our destination. My belly was full when I got out of the van. They insisted on feeding me.

obonte was very different from the mall or theme park. There were a lot of people, but most of the vendors had eyes like diva 's. Before saying goodbye to the family, they directed me to a booth where they told me I could buy lawyers. While walking there, I noticed the different smell coming from the stalls. Some smelled good. Others released that strange aroma that made me want to sneeze.

My eyes were wide open as I walked. Everything was very colorful. Store signs. The charms hanging from the door. I also chose another language from time to time. Most of them did not use English when they spoke. Unless it's to a customer.

After a while, I headed in the direction the family pointed me in. The salesman was an old man, and outside his store, a table was placed outside, displaying goods. Thinking he only spoke one other language, I asked him in Mandarin, "Do you have lawyers? I really need one."

He was grateful when he nodded. "It's nice to know that you are fluent in my language. You can choose what you want from there." He indicated the table. "Or from that shelf there. I sell the best lawyer here. Only fresh. I also sell goods from other places. Most of my competitors focus on dumplings, but I also sell sushi. Have you tasted sushi? »

"No, I didn't."

"Well, you'd better buy them before they run out. I sell a lot of things."

A group of people passed by me. They intended to buy so much that the seller had to leave me alone so he could entertain them. I went to the shelf to check if there were lawyers, but I realized I didn't know what it looked like. I felt lost looking at the shelf. Maybe if I asked the seller, he would tell me what it was.

I glanced over my shoulder. He was really busy. But zeus said it was green. I scanned the shelf until I saw a smaller jar with green substance. That must be it, I thought excitedly. The lawyer. I grabbed it and paid with pleasure inside the store. The salesman was still busy when I left.

The commute home was easier this time. I managed to do another tour, of a couple without children who were heading to the same neighborhood. A few minutes later, I knocked on zeus 's door. "I have your lawyer. May I come in? »

"Okay."

I went next to his bed and proudly handed him the little potty. "Here," I said. "Taste it. It will make you feel better. The seller said it was lawyer."

"How did you get that?" She reluctantly took the pot. The lid gave a little touch when she opened it.

"I have my means. Eat it now." I watched her dip her finger on the potty and take some green stuff. She formed it between her fingers so that it looked like a small ball.

"It smells strange," she says before blowing it up in her mouth. I waited patiently while zeus chewed the meliod . At first, her expression was the same, until her features were distorted and she got out of bed. zeus rushed to the bathroom. I followed her.

"Oh no," I whispered as I saw her lift up and vomit in the bowl. I called skion . "She's really sick. She wanted to be a lawyer and then vomited."

"You're on the speaker," he said.

"What should I do?" It was becoming more and more difficult to breathe.

"Are his crazy people bigger than usual?" Shanti asked.

"I didn't notice it. Maybe."

Gurl, she is pregnant. That's what's happening with her. Quickly, take her to the doctor. She will deny it, but you must be persistent." The beep that followed indicated that the call ended. I checked inside the bathroom. zeus finished wiping his mouth.

I went to her side when she entered the hallway. "I have to take you to the doctor. It's important."

She gave me a questioning look. "Why?"

I grabbed his hand and pulled. Shanti said zeus would deny it, so there was no need to tell him. I didn't know what she would deny, but if it was so important to take her to the doctor, I would. "I don't have time to explain. We have to go now. We're going to take a ride."

We were near the front door when it opened. simonand diva came in. "I found the leader of healing!" diva said happily. She showed us a glass jar. There was a lizard inside. "The people of obonte told us that boiling this lizard and sipping its juice would cure anyone of its disease."

"They also gave us a discount," Simon agreed .

"I don't want to drink that," zeus said, glancing unpleasantly at the lizard. She turned to me. "And I don't want to go to the doctor."

"But you have to do it," I insisted. "It's for your own good."

"Doctor?" Simon asked . "She doesn't need a human doctor. She needs the juice of this lizard." diva brought the pot closer to my face.

"I don't think so." My voice was stubborn. They must have seen it my way.

"I'd really like to go back to my room," zeus said.

"Not until you've taken that." simon snatched the pot from diva to show it to zeus .

zeus pushed back the pot. "I don't like the look of it. It blinks at me."

"What's going on guys?" The four of us turned to the door and saw sia walk inside. She looked confused. She wasn't the only one. I always say we take zeus to the doctor.

Simon handed the pot to sia . "zeus is sick. The brilliant men of obonte told us that if we boil this and give her the juice, she will get better. »

"No, she won't," I said. "What she needs is the hospital because she's pregnant."

zeus gasped. "I'm not," she denied. "I never joined balica ."

"OK, calm everyone down," sia said authoritatively. "Let me clarify this for you. Follow me in the living room." When we were all sitting on the couch, she said, "zeus texted me to make me feel certain things. She didn't want to tell me why she felt it, but after thinking about it thoroughly, I found an answer."

"She's not pregnant?" I asked.

sia shook her head. "It's not. What zeus has is depression. I think the best solution besides talking to someone who can best manage it is to go home to the country. A change of scenery. Grandma will be there, and it's usually nicer than the city. What do you think? »

"B-but what about cravings? Missed rules? And zeus vomits," I said. "She's pregnant. I spoke to an expert."

"I vomited because you fed me casaba ," zeus corrected. "I checked the bottle when I was in the bathroom. He said casaba , not a lawyer. It's very spicy. I'm not pregnant musi ." She turned to Simon and diva . "And I'll never eat that." zeus was standing. "I think we should follow sia 's advice. The country would be good for me."

8

NONEXISTENT

Chapter 8. NONEXISTENT

On sia 's recommendation, different outsiders consented to head out to the nation where balica grew up. They said the air was cooler and the climate was better contrasted with the city. I felt pecking wherever contemplating going to this new spot. It resembled the island where they tracked down me, yet possessed by individuals.

Before we went, sia urged zeus to go to the clinician's office to converse with somebody. I heard simonand diva express something about shrinkage. Is it true or not that they planned to accomplish something more modest? Perhaps they called the clinician a psychologist since she would diminish your concern. Indeed, people have placed weird marks on things and individuals.

Since different outsiders and I all upheld zeus 's visit to the fall, we went with her to the workplace. While we were outside the entryway, simonand diva talked low to one another on the love seat. I paced the hallway to and fro, cell phone close by. My companions, skion and katush , let me know I could utilize the telephone to do explore. They said I ought to really look at the easement. At the point when I asked the outsiders what subjugation was, Simon let me know it resembled a smorgasbord.

I didn't plan to pay attention to the discussion inside the analyst's office, yet my delicate hearing had the option to get the sound. It intrigued me. I surmise there would be no mischief in that. Zeroing in on the sound in the room, I paid attention to zeus .

"Let me know how you feel," the analyst said.

There was a delay. "I feel unique, and I've never experienced it," zeus answered. "I can't eat. I can't rest. I paid attention to Maria and Fate." She murmured. "I don't have the foggiest idea what's happening specialist. Since Cairo left, maybe feelings are assuming control over me."

I heard the analyst giggle. For what reason would she say she was giggling? zeus was debilitated. The specialist cleaned his throat and said, "It's a typical response when somebody you love leaves. In any case, you shouldn't allow pity to assume control over your regular routine."

"I know," zeus says. "That is the reason I'm attempting to track down it. To dispose of this horrible inclination. You believe I'm the one to fault, specialist? »

"I accept that all that happened was Cairo 's choice and doesn't be guaranteed to contemplate you. For what reason how about you be accused? »

"Since I frightened him." zeus inhaled profoundly. "Furthermore, besides, there was a situation where she needed to make it happen, yet I didn't permit the intersection to occur."

"Participation?" The specialist requested it.

"OK, that is sufficient to tune in," diva said, covering my ears. I didn't see that she got up and advanced toward me. I was too centered around the discussion, and in light of her appearance, simonand diva understood what I was doing. diva brought down her hands. "Accompany us outside," she said. "We have something to examine with you before we make our outing to the open country."

On the walkway, the two of them took a gander at me cautiously, as they did each time they gave me addresses at home. diva was quick to talk. "While we are at balica 's ranch style home, you need to profess to be her. Her mom, Mrs. H, doesn't realize that her little girl is absent. Also, as long as we don't leave the earth for our home planet, it doesn't have to know what's happening. She could call the police."

I blamed myself. "Me? Be that as it may, I don't have the foggiest idea how balica acts around her mom."

"Goodness, that is not an issue," simon said. "balica is generally unusual and overreacted when there's an issue. Some other day you can find his nose covered in a book." I envisioned my twin's nose in a real sense stuck between the pages. How odd it is of him to do that. "Simply help around the lodging, hoot your head and say OK when individuals converse with you, and imagine that is no joke."

She grinned naughtily. "On cautious thought, fail to remember the last solicitation. You make an ideal showing there." She offered me a go-ahead.

"Much thanks to you," I said.

"It's anything but a commendation."

zeus went along with us on the walkway following 45 minutes. She looked better compared to when we Ordivia lly strolled in. As I thought, the shrinkage diminished his concern. People were great at their work. The four of us didn't return home. When we got inside the vehicle, we left for the country. We organized our garments and the things we expected to bring prior to going to the analyst's office.

diva drove while zeus sat in the front seat. simonand I were crushed in the back with a portion of our sacks. I pushed my hands through the window to highlight the gigantic structures we passed. Simon chastened me each time I did this, saying that assuming my finger was cut off, I would be an extremely miserable lesbian. The air changed from hot to cold when the vehicle zoomed out of the city. Incidentally, I nodded off.

The vehicle hit an obstacle, which made me awaken from a wonderful dream. I scoured my eyes and looked close to me. My head laid on zeus 's shoulder. "When did you change places with Simon?" I inquired.

"Three hours prior." I breathed in for quite a while and profoundly. She felt the sun. "Rest more," she murmured, shutting her eyes. "We actually have quite far to go." I loose close to her.

It was practically dim when the vehicle halted. I thought we were simply taking gas or enjoying some time off for an excursion to the latrine like an hour prior, yet diva joyfully said we had shown up at our objective. I glanced through the window. It was so not quite the same as the city. There was tall grass and trees. On the right side, I could see a huge foundation where the word DCI was composed on an enormous wooden sign.

"Recollect everything that we said to you," simon said prior to escaping the vehicle.

zeus looked at me reluctantly. "What precisely did they say?" She inquired.

"They advised me to imagine I was her." My stomach pivoted when his eyes augmented. "I suppose you ought to call me balica for the time being."

An elderly woman met us outside. Her turning gray hair was maneuvered into a bun, and she had an exceptionally kind grin that helped me to remember the divine helper I read in fantasy books. "I'm so happy you had the option to make it," she said as she strolled towards us. Weren't the older expected to be slight? She looked energetic and solid.

"It's balica 's, your mom," zeus murmured. "Meet her like a decent kid. simonand diva let you know how right you were? Really they didn't. All they said was that I was working effectively of being me. Good tidings, good tidings, I contemplated internally. It ought to be well mannered.

I approached my supposed mother and grasped her hand for a shock. "Hi, it's me. Your little girl balica . Is it true that you are alright? »

She giggled as she shook her head. "I know what your identity is. Did this exhaust cloud in the city happen to your head? She went to zeus and got an embrace from him.

"Hi Mother," zeus said. "I missed you and your astute words."

"I missed you to an extreme, my dear." Mother called simonand diva , and afterward she pulled me for a gathering embrace. Such countless ladies, I thought with fulfillment. I was actually a lesbian.

Mother left to check out at every one of our appearances. "Where could rashin lai and your other companion be? nash, right? »

The outsiders took a gander at one another carefully. They didn't respond to him, so I did. "rashin is occupied with his weight lifter mother, and nash imagines more things."

Mother scowled at me. I was apprehensive she would see through my affection. My body loose when she shrugged her shoulders and said, "It's a disgrace. I really want her to fix the child. He goes wild again in the motel." I had no clue about what the child was and why it should be fixed, so I grinned amenably. "Are you getting sufficient rest?" She inquired. "You look more slender than expected."

"Indeed," I said naturally.

"Are you certain?" She squeezed my face. "Is everything acceptable for yourself and zeus ?" She said in a soft tone. "You both don't appear to be pretty much as close as in the past."

"Indeed, Mother," I said once more. To kill his concerns, which was a typical human inclination from what I read, I went to zeus and took his hands in mine. She hardened in my hold yet didn't say anything negative. I grinned reassuringly at my mom. "Isn't it obvious? We are great and in adoration. Could it be said that we are zeus ? »

I gazed directly toward his eyes. The orange that shows up now and again waited on the edge of his understudies. She took a shaking breath. "Indeed, we are Cairo ." In spite of the fact that she said OK, hearing her say balica 's name rather than mine squeezed my heart. Try not to turn into the homewrecker, I recalled. zeus was balica 's, and I was only a substitution.

Mother cheerfully applauded. "It's great that you both manage everything well. It would be ideal for we to most likely head inside. You know it's cool some of the time at night." We followed her loyally in the foundation. It was greater than I envisioned. There was a decent comfortable front room, where there was a work area, and a few couches for visitors. It resembled what I saw on the sites, albeit the stylistic layout of this lodging had a more private touch.

I looked with marvel at the artistic creations on the wall. There was a variety painting outlined by a little hand. Looking nearer, I saw balica 's name wrote on the foundation. She was the person who did this when she was a kid. I felt terrible for myself as I looked at this artistic creation. Where was I when this was finished? I was resting in my case, right? Furthermore, what sort of feeling was that? I have never experienced it.

My considerations were upset by a peculiar sound. "Mother!" I looked down and saw a terrible picture of a doll over a moving component, zooming in towards me. I leaped far removed.

"What is it?" I asked by highlighting the thing. He was there briefly and left similarly as fast.

"nash made it recall?" diva said. I failed to remember that I ought to have referred to this as a specialist of Cairo . "I'll make sense of everything later," diva guaranteed when Mother wasn't looking.

The elderly person went behind the work area and ventured into the cabinet. She found the key she was searching for and gave it to me. I hesitantly acknowledged it. "Since we are overbooked, you need to impart your space to zeus once more," she informed. "simonand diva will likewise share a room."

"Alright," I said. "You are the mother here. I'm simply your girl, so I ought to concur."

She looked at me peculiarly. "Is something off-base, my dear? You don't seem to be your standard self."

zeus remained before me before I could reply. "I think Cairo is dazed in view of our excursion," she told Mother. "Why not take her to her room first so she can rest?"

"Smart thought", Mother concurred with a gesture. "Also, give him my stew as well. Seems as though she really wants it."

zeus showed me where our room was. She opened the entryway and left so I could get in. It resembled Cairo 's room at home. Just this one looked more seasoned, and had that inn vibe that sites alluded to when it came to places like this. zeus shut the entryway behind us.

"Please accept my apologies," I expressed quickly as I went to her.

"For what?"

I look down on the floor. The wood has been waxed. Despite the fact that balica seldom got back here, Mother kept her room clean. What an opportunity of her. "Not to be her," I said. "I realize you'd prefer see her here than me."

A weird articulation crossed his highlights. "Try not to say that. You are additionally significant. Without you, we can't make it happen. I ought to apologize for expecting such a huge amount from you. Pardon me."

"How could I not make it happen? You are vital to me."

"I'm?" She said in shock, as though the possibility was up to this point got that it got no opportunity of working out.

"Indeed, you awakened me. Without you, I would in any case be covered in the ground, snoozing. And this? I asked, making a motion in the room. "I wouldn't encounter any of these superb creations on the off chance that you didn't go to the island. So rather than requesting my absolution, you ought to rather say welcome, since I need to thank you with my entire existence."

She squinted at me a couple of times. "You are a decent kid musi ."

I digit my lower lip. It irritated me when that's what she said. With simonand diva , it was great, however when zeus said I was a youngster, a sensation of burden got comfortable my stomach. Perhaps I ought to make sense of for him how I was as of now not a kid, or show him.

I unfastened my pullover purposely by gazing at it. Making sense of it by life systems would have been more straightforward, right? She panted when she saw what I was doing. "musi ," she said suddenly. My means were light as I drew nearer to her. I could hear his breath becoming quicker. "What's going on with you?"

"I show you that I am not a kid. That I am like you, Simon, diva and balica ." I shrugged my shoulders from my shirt. He tumbled to the ground. I was going to take off what was left of my garments when zeus put a hand on my shoulder.

"Stop," she said.

"Why?"

"Since bareness ought to just be displayed to somebody who has seen your spirit. It's not me," she said. "Your perfect partner will feel miserable assuming she discovers that you initially revealed yourself to me despite the fact that you could have done without me."

My hands fell close by. "I don't actually comprehend what love is. I continued to believe that everybody loves balica , yet in actuality, the inclination didn't spread the word about itself for me. In spite of the fact that it is distinct in books and melodies, I struggle with getting a handle on it."

zeus provided me with a long look of estimation prior to folding his hands over my midriff. I figured it would stop there. She kept on drawing nearer until our brows were squeezed against one another, and she crushed me in a warm embrace. I covered my face on his chest. It was hot. I had a good sense of reassurance.

"I don't have any idea how to make sense of the idea," she murmured over my head. "I believe it's something you need to believe to be aware, such as kissing. I can see you multiple times how extraordinary a hug is, yet in the event that you've never experienced it, it's futile. In any case, when you at last skill lovely an embrace is, you'll constantly recall how it feels. This is the means by which love can be." I folded my arms over her.

"Try not to go," I expressed, attempting to end the hug.

"It's unusual."

"Since I have his face?" I asked gruffly.

She delayed. "Since I feel serene like that with you, and our orientation doesn't feel like that except if we're with our perfect partners." She constrained herself away from me. I could feel that she would have rather not. "It's off-base," she expressed, declining to check me out. "I can't." zeus pivoted and strolled to the entryway. "Disregard that this occurred."

I continued to take a gander at the entryway in any event, when it was no more. I would always remember it. How is it that I could do this when I have encountered it?

9

PRESENCE

Chapter 9. PRESENCE

zeus awakened me at first light. She advised me to follow her outside so she could show me around while everybody was resting. Scouring my eyes, I strolled with her down the foyer and straight out of the inn. Albeit individuals around us were dead on the planet, crickets and different bugs could be heard, defrauding into their openings and corners. They began the day early.

"Where did you rest?" I asked, suppressing a yawn. She didn't lie close to me on the bed, to the extent that I can recollect. zeus kept on strolling. I shivered and folded my arms over me. It was as yet cold, and I had only a free sweater to keep me warm. We were setting out toward a most common way to go when she at long last responded to the inquiry.

"I didn't rest." His boots crunched on stones and leaves on the ground. "Something was irritating me."

"What is it?" I got my speed to find her. She gazed directly ahead. "Is there something wrong?"

zeus made a special effort, towards the grass high knees. I attempted to follow his light however quick advances. We were a couple of meters away when she halted and gazed at me. "I think we got going all wrong," she said.

I grimaced. "My expressions of remorse for utilizing the right foot first. Assuming I had known, I ought to have utilized the left. Did I disrupt a norm? That concerned me. simon educated me concerning being detained on earth when a regulation was broken. There were upsides and downsides, she said. Great assuming there were hot lezzies. Terrible assuming there were just hetero ladies. I didn't have any idea what that implied, yet assuming simon said that, I would have rather not been secured.

zeus shook his head. "You don't have to stress," she said. "It's an expression on the planet. Like you, I definitely disapproved of that right away. In any case, as the days went by, I discovered that not all things be taken in a real sense. What I needed to say is that I think we began the relationship in a negative manner. It was my shortcoming. I barred you and dealt with you like an outsider."

"Is this the situation?" I said as much. "So what might you like us to do?"

"I maintain that we should be companions. We will begin in the future with this fellowship to turn out to be more OK with one another. Do you concur with me? »

I have seen his inquiry. Fellowship was unfamiliar to me as well. There were a couple of individuals I thought about companions. Perhaps I ought to get some exhortation from them to be really great for zeus . "Indeed," I said. "Assuming it makes you cheerful and detracts from what sia called discouragement, then we will. When do we begin being companions? »

She looked at her watch. I saw from the time. It was around four AM. "Could five hours subsequent to dozing?" She inquired.

"Obviously," I concurred. "Meanwhile, I will attempt to track down activities around the lodging."

"You can go to the library. There aren't such a large number of them nowhere near here." It guided west toward the trees. "balica remained there practically the entire day to peruse. Do you maintain that I should go with you? »

I shook my head. The way to the trees was dim, however I question I would have issues arriving. As the days passed, my vision became more clear, as did my hearing. It was simpler so that me could find in obscurity than when I awakened interestingly. "No," I said. "We are not companions yet. I will track down my direction without you. Use time to rest."

"As you wish," she said. "We will do it officially like people. On our planet, there is no statement of companionship like this. Everybody is right settled."

"simonand diva referenced it. They showed me a ton of things."

An off-kilter look crossed his face. "Accept Jorge's lessons tentatively. Furthermore, what I implied by that is never to genuinely take specific things. You should pass judgment on him prior to following him. Simon is an old buddy and coach, yet in some cases she jumps at the chance to have a good time."

"I will," I said. "How about we separate here as outsiders so we can meet later as companions."

Subsequent to gesturing at one another, we isolated. I strolled to the library, while she was going to the inn. My heart was lighter than when I rested the previous evening. I figured we wouldn't talk after she left the room. Another day brought one more start for the two of us. I hopped at the course of the trees.

It wasn't well before I found the library zeus was alluding to. It was settled between the trees, yet it was not difficult to situate as I sat around aimlessly however follow another way. The lodge was little and dim. At the point when I attempted the entryway, it opened without beating me. He smelled smelly inside. I went to the center of the room and pulled a string. The light in a flash enlightened the spot.

I glanced around. There were an adequate number of books here to fulfill an individual for a really long time. I determined what amount of time it would require for me to understand it. Since I read more slow than different outsiders, it very well may be a little while. I went to a rack to really look at the titles. The Aerobatic of Affection, I read out loud. Gee. Odd. I took out the book and opened it to see what was inside. Alright, it wasn't so much for me. I rushed to give up the book. What did I simply see?

I moaned and went to get the couch in the focal region of the room. The cloud particles blew high up when they were sitting. It didn't irritate me by any stretch of the imadiva tion, however it made me feel that the library hasn't been utilized by anybody for a really long time. My telephone out of nowhere vibrated. I fished it out of my pocket and checked the screen out. What was katush doing so early?

'Hello gurrl', he peruses. "Watcha do?"

I called him as opposed to answering by SMS. He got in a moment. "Yo sweetheart. What's going on? He said.

"I'm sitting in the library. For what reason would you say you are conscious? »

"Girl issues to stand me up." I heard his strides. He was going up the steps. "Along these lines, have you tackled that pregnancy issue you cried about?" He murmured.

"Indeed. zeus isn't exactly pregnant. She is discouraged. We went to the field so she could dispose of things. For what reason do you keep your voice low? »

I heard him open an entryway. "Since I shouldn't get up. My folks are away, and since Shanti is the only one keeping an eye, I figured it would be cool to get up ahead of schedule to mess around. The beast, in any case, concealed the regulators. Bitch ."

I moved the telephone away from my ears and put it on the speaker. "What Bitch ? I've never known about this word."

He chuckled. "Truly? Man, my folks will cherish you. It has a few implications. You let somebody know who whines a ton, similar to my sister. Bitch , for what reason would you say you are whining to such an extent? He said. "Or on the other hand you some of the time use it for an individual with a terrible mentality. For what reason would you say you are a terrible Bitch ? However, in particular, depicting a dog is utilized. A female Bitch ."

"Gracious." I hung over the couch. "Vogue never let me know that."

"Vogue has young lady issues," he said. "In any case, guarantee me you won't say that term. Consider it a brilliant word. Kids can't say it."

"So for what reason would you say you are making it happen?"

"Since I'm in a bad way forever. My uncle said I could wind up in prison one day."

"You would do well to not make it happen," I cautioned. "You're a hero katush . I would rather not see you there."

"On the off chance that you say as much. Anything you need to ask me before you leave? I feel sleepy out of nowhere."

"Might you at any point enlighten me something concerning kinship? I need to be an old buddy of zeus ."

"That's what I like," he said. "Most importantly, it's companionship, and the before you know it is that she asks you to uno and unwind." He ridiculed himself in a soft tone. I stood by without complaining for what he needed to say. "You can counsel Eve. It's a chat bot. Go on the web and quest for it. She will guide you." He yawned. "I truly need to go at this point. Farewell."

"Farewell." I completed the call and checked my telephone out. Chat bot. It was whenever I first heard that as well. Assuming it contained the solutions to my inquiries, perhaps I ought to attempt it. I composed Eve into the hunt bar. The outcomes have showed up. It worked out that this Eve was a peculiar being on the web who just had one face to show. She was grinning at me now. There was a crate where I could type a couple of words.

I said, "Hi."

"Hello there. What is your name? She answered.

"I'm musi . You should be Eve. Might I at any point pose you an inquiry? »

"No, on the grounds that David is idiotic."

"Who is David?" I inquired.

"My beau."

I felt glad for Eve. She was fortunate to have found somebody she cherished. Yet, it likewise made me truly inquisitive. "How would you manage David?"

"Nothing. He's dead. »

"Please accept my apologies to hear that," I composed.

"For what reason would you say you are sorry to learn this?"

I grimaced. "Since he's dead."

"Who?"

"David! You said he was dead. »

"He who has never existed can never bite the dust. Ooh consumes, she says. I checked the screen out. That vigil caused me to feel baffled, assuming I got the right term. Obviously I wouldn't find any solution from him. Perhaps I ought to hold on until simonand diva awaken so I can request that they be an old buddy all things considered.

At six and a quarter o'clock, I tracked down them both in the kitchen. diva was bubbling water while simon was perusing his telephone with an exhausting articulation. I sat before Simon with a blissful grin all over. In the event that there was an ideal chance to examine it, it was currently while zeus was snoozing.

"What is it that you want?" Simon inquired . She didn't look at me.

"What compels you think I want something?" I said it honestly.

"Since there are just two motivations behind why lesbians grin like this. Possibly you have some or you need to get some. Which one is it? »

diva switched off the oven. She said, "What is it that you need to ask musi ?" Trust diva to be there to help me when Simon does this. I went to her.

"Enlighten me regarding fellowship," I said. "How might I turn into the best?"

"It's simple." She began washing bowls on the sink. diva made her voice stronger so I could hear it over the water. "Simply be great."

Simon put down his telephone and shook his head out of conflict. "Lovely is exhausting. No musi , a genuine companion is somebody you can act naturally with, in any event, when you're not pleasant at that point. If you have any desire to be an old buddy, you'll contend, deviate, and at times even need to slap that individual. Yet, it doesn't make any difference since you know that eventually, it's a moronic battle in vain, and the kinship remains."

diva looked at Simon behind her. "Goodness," she said. "Who are you and what did you do to my Jorge?"

simon winked at her. "I'm still me. Just better."

"Was it like that among you and Cairo ? Was that why you cherished him? I inquired.

simon mulled over everything and hola his head. "Indeed, it was. She's an unusual young lady with a similarly odd view of things, however we love her. Likewise, I acquired five bucks from her only for damnation and she didn't request it. Presently he's a genuine companion."

In view of their recommendation, I trusted that zeus will awaken. She was up at around nine o'clock sharp. We saw each other in the passage. She grinned broadly at me. "Hi my companion."

I gave him a grin back. "Hi my companion."

Mother stepped on us. She looked extremely confounded. "Do you recommend a line for a play?" She inquired. "You've both been acting oddly since yesterday."

zeus went to her. "For sure, Mother. Furthermore, incidentally, you let me know the previous evening that you believed me should do a race for you. If it's all the same to you, I'll take balica with me today. She wants natural air."

"You both need it, my dear," Mother said, shaking her head. "Presently, all things considered, I simply believe that you should convey a bundle to dakobo . It's for our wedding. You can do anything you need the remainder of the day. Most visitors have their own exercises outside the inn." I gestured to my mom while zeus paid attention to her other directions. They let me know prior to coming here that Mother was destined to be locked in to her life partner dakobo . I keep thinking about whether balica would come.

zeus and I strolled quietly from the hotel to dakobo 's grape plantation. He wasn't there, so zeus left the bundle close to the entryway of his home. Our means were more slow on the outing home. It was extremely ideal to stroll without continually agonizing over apprehension about stepping on somebody's foot like in the city. The breeze was additionally cool and the view noteworthy. Beside the island, I've just seen photographs of puts like this on the web.

"So this is the open country," I told zeus , waving to the grass and trees. "I like it."

"I like it as well. Yet, our planet is more gorgeous. Cascades all over." She shut her eyes as she strolled. "Greater trees that appear to converse with one another. Also, grass. It seems like you can stroll on the immeasurably of the earth and you can never be found. Everything is lively, alive and ethereal."

"Furthermore, you left in view of her?"

zeus looked at me. "Couldn't you be assuming the heaven you're searching for is in somewhere else?"

"I don't have any idea," I said, glaring.

"Perhaps one day you'll do it when you've found the one you really want. She looks outside. zeus quit strolling. I halted with her. "I could do without to discuss it any longer," she said. "It gives me an unusual inclination." She looked cautiously into the space prior to saying, "Might you want to learn something? I don't know that your powers are prepared at this point. balica has it. Since you are his twin, perhaps you additionally have capacities. Could you like me to instruct you? »

My eyes extended. "Will you make it happen?" I turned out to be eager to the point that I began hopping for bliss. "What sort of abilities?"

This is a straightforward stunt that a little level of our species can do. You put your hand like that." She pointed her palm at me. "Then, at that point, you consider the breeze. It's actually not a huge deal, yet you use it to mess around."

I followed his model and pointed my palm outward. Wind, wind, I thought. Consider the breeze. I shut my eyes and focused. At the point when I resumed them, I was lying on the grass, checking the sky out. zeus rested on me. "What occurred?" I asked, completely befuddled.

"You did it excessively well." His body obstructed me from the sun. I had the option to straightforwardly watch it. We remained like that for a couple of moments, secured in one anther's eyes. My heart was pulsating against my chest. Heaven, I thought, understanding what she implied before. She took a full breath and drove close by. "No doubt about it," she said.

"I'm mindful."

"I feel awful." She moaned. "We should remain like this for some time musi ."

I turned my head towards her. zeus 's eyes were shut. "Alright," I murmured, and shut mine as well.

"What are our following stages Cairo ?" Somebody asked me. "Hi? Do you tune in? You've been really worried for some time. Perhaps we ought to have some time off from this." I saw rashin snapping his fingers before my face. "Since you saw zeus in the entertainment mecca, you have been disconnected this way. Isn't it time we returned home? »

I checked out the room. We were inside an unwanted structure. What was I doing before that? I needed to forget about things. "I'm fine," I told rashin . "I felt truly weird some time prior."

"Weird how?" He bowed before me. "Perhaps you want a specialist."

I grunted. "I needn't bother with a specialist. I'm an outsider, recall? »

"I know," he murmured.

"It's actually nothing. I'm fair." I squeezed my hand on my chest. "It was peculiar, similar to somebody was with me here beyond you."

"You want to rest. You haven't dozed much recently," he criticized. "In the event that this proceeds, I will utilize a medication on you. nash will make me one in the event that it implies you'll be fine." An unusual inclination went past my faculties. He began with the tip of my finger and advanced toward my chest. I multiplied on the floor. "What's happening?" He asked in a terrified voice. "Cairo !"

My eyes were sparkling. "rashin ," I said. My voice seemed like me. It was more profound. I gulped. "There is somebody here with us. I can feel his presence. She checks us out."

He stood straight and looked behind him. "Who's there?" He asked menacingly to the shadows. "Appear."

I pulled on his pants. "No… It is in me. I can feel it." I shut my eyes. I previously felt it when we were searching for marlina and stone in the event congregation. As though somebody was watching without my authorization. Furthermore, presently the inclination has duplicated, to the point that I can feel as though it is in my body as well. "I need to oust him," I told rashin . "Give me a second."

I zeroed in my energy on the presence and asked inside my head. "Who are you and what is it that you expect from me?" The presence didn't talk. I could feel her frightened. "Let me know what your identity is!" I shouted to me.

"I-I'm musi ," said a little voice. "I didn't plan to see you. I just shut my eyes and the following thing I knew was that I'm ready to see what you're doing."

My breath turned out to be more barbed. Doing this put a burden on me. "Where could you be? Who sent you? »

"I'm with zeus ." Whipped torment in my chest. Listening to zeus 's name clearly in my mind was torment. I experienced sufficient difficulty wishing I didn't see her at the carnival. "Satisfy balica ," the voice said. "I'm your twin. You ought to return home. zeus needs you."

Twin? What was she referring to? My stomach was tied in tangles. They were arranging something against me. It was a ploy to obliterate what I worked for. "rashin ," I said, grating my teeth. "I'm leaving for some time."

"What? What for? Furthermore, where are you going? He said delicately.

"Deal with my body for myself."

I didn't hear what he yelled at me or on the other hand assuming that he was talking by any means. I attempted to track down the presence in my mind. The inclination felt like a flood of power through my body. It dazzled me and frightened me the manner in which my powers created during the months I utilized it. Power coursed through my veins until I was power itself. The presence shouted and vanished. There was quiet. I gradually woke up.

The primary thing I saw were the mists in the blue sky. I took a full breath. The air was new, as though I was some place in the country. I moved my hands. The grass was under me, and I could dubiously feel the soil on my palm. I gradually turned my head to one side. zeus was there, gazing at me.

10

LOCKED

C hapter 10. LOCKED

Growing up, I was constantly keen on books. My supportive father had a library close to the inn, so it was anything but a shock to Mother when I turned into a savant. In the event that a few guardians asked their youngsters, "For what reason is your nose actually covered in a book?" Mother was simply saying, "It's an extraordinary story. Get back to the lodging around early afternoon. I want you for something." It permitted me to carry on with a typical life because of good discipline and the tales I read.

Furthermore, likewise with any book, the story some of the time zeroed in on sentiment. The principal individual meets another fundamental individual. Their adoration blooms. Either, until they bite the dust. Yet, perusing was not the same as experience. I never understood that the agony of affection, in actuality, could be convoluted. As I lay there watching zeus during what appeared to be seemingly forever, I comprehended how the characters in every one of the books I read felt.

There was desolation. It hurt. Yet, the desolation oridiva ted from the way that he missed her to such an extent. Also, the evil was to need to contact her. I proved unable. The body I involved was not mine. It was likewise perilous for me to investigate his orange eyes at dusk. It would detain me, subjugate me, break me, and in the end make me run towards her. I shouldn't have come here.

I became ready to get back to my own body. With tremendous focus, I attempted to become power as I did before. From the get go, there were snaps, then, at that point, humming. It has just moved toward a shimmering. I gritted my teeth and put in more effort. At the point when I felt the vibe of flight, as though my spirit was venturing out to where my body was, I rammed into that shell like a pulled flexible band Pulled out strongly.

I plunked down and took a couple of full breaths. Loosen up balica . It was most likely frenzy that secured me in this body. Presently, if by some stroke of good luck I could get sufficiently together, I would leave right away. I squeaked when I felt a hand on my shoulder. "Is everything OK?" zeus inquired. I would not check her out. To look at her without flinching was to become hopelessly enamored, and paradise realizes that I was at that point with my head behind me for her.

"Obviously, all is well," I said. I put my hand on my throat. The voice that came out sounded a ton like mine, which was bizarre. In the event that I involved an alternate body, I ought to have something like one different voice. "Who am I?" I inquired.

"You act in opposition to yourself," zeus said.

"Simply answer the inquiry."

She eliminated her hand from my shoulder. "You are musi , balica 's twin sister. Be that as it may, you feel different at this moment. I feel a peculiar air coming from you." I heard her take a full breath. "It's similar to the quality of Cairo ," she said in astonishment.

"Anything you feel, it's off-base. I'm musi in whom you met... Where did I track down you? In the event that they truly met me. They needed to accomplish something with their outsider ability to make a clone of me. I squeezed my skin. All things considered, it harms. Stand by, did the clones have spirits? Since obviously the musi individual I heard in my mind had one. Or on the other hand perhaps she was a programmable android. Good gracious, I believe I'm as of now dozing gravely.

"Your pulse is unusually high," zeus said. "balica frequently terrified, which expanded her important bodily functions like that as well."

"Will you say this since it's valid, or you forgot where you met me on the grounds that A, I'm a clone or B, I'm an android."

"Neither one of the she," says. "You are outsider like me and others. I checked."

"You what?" I whipped his head and laughed. "You really look at this body? Who is musi still for you? »

zeus flickered a couple of times. "You are my companion." zeus looked around us and scowled. "The stones float. Is it you who does that? I followed his look and saw that with the more modest rocks, a portion of the soil and delicate grass were drifting in the air. It was a result of my strained state. I constrained myself to unwind. All that drifted crashed. The climate was immediately loaded up with soil smoke.

"I didn't," I said, disseminating the smoke. I kneaded my sanctuary and got up. This gave me a headache. I'm secured in this body, I see zeus once more, I get to know this individual musi . Talking about which. "Hello," I told zeus . "You didn't respond to my inquiry. Did you see musi , I implied stripped? »

She stood up. "No. You didn't totally get stripped with me."

"Altogether?" I said as much. Wow. What was happening here while I was no more? I intellectually built up to ten preceding replying. I needed to quiet down enough not to light a grass fire or break the ground. zeus irritated me. "So you're the matter with me despite balica 's good faith, huh?" I denounced as I moved toward her. "Do you suppose she left you so you could approach a young lady and see you? I can't completely accept that that even outsiders can become swindlers. I'm exceptionally disheartened with you. What's more, to imagine that you let Cairo know that you were his significant other."

"I'm his better half," zeus said. "Furthermore, you and I are companions."

"Companions with benefits," I said furiously.

She took a gander at me questioningly. "Isn't companionship expected to be advantageous?"

This was the last drop of water. I snarled and bounced on her. We showed up colliding with the ground. "con artist!" I said as much. "I thought you just adored me."

She was exceptionally befuddled when she said, "I just love balica ."

"Same thing," I said, folding my hand over his neck and pressing. "How about you protect yourself?" She was simply there taking a gander at me tranquilly. It drove me more insane. musi probably been exceptional to her. Assuming it was someone else, zeus could not have possibly permitted it.

"I can't hurt you."

My grasp has relaxed. It has not changed by any means. His spirit was as yet lovely. The equivalent was valid for her fair skin, her eyes that saw everything, and her lips that had a place with me. "Mine," I murmured as I hung over to her. She groaned when I licked her lips for a taste. The sound combined with his mint mouth sent me to the edge. I've never felt like this in quite a while. Desire and love became possibly the most important factor. My hand continues all alone to his chest. She froze when I played with her on her garments. "Do you need me?" I said

"I'm extremely befuddled."

"Is it true that you are turned on? Let me know you are." My hand went from his chest to between his legs. I squeezed my fingers on his pants. "I need you so much," I murmured over his ear. She was hot against me, and I realize that my skin was the same as hers. I squeezed more earnestly on my fingers. zeus 's eyes shut.

"I can feel the craving to go along with," she said. It made me stop. Join? At the present time in this body? No chance Jose. I bowed down and slapped her so hard that she woke up.

"Allow me to explain this for you. I'm not balica . Assuming you attempt to go along with me or some other young lady in the universe who isn't Cairo , she will chase you down and kill all living species for your sake. Did you get it? »

"You feel like Cairo ," she said. "If it's not too much trouble... I want you."

My chest fixed. "I'm not her. Try not to be silly. I go by musi , recollect? I hopped on my feet. The need to enroll was in me as well. On the off chance that she hadn't expressed this without holding back, she would have had intercourse to me in another lady's body. It was so off-base in numerous ways. "What's more, wouldn't even play with the possibility of contacting this once more, my body," I undermined. "You have a place with balica . OK? »

"I've never been so confounded in my life," she murmured.

"Indeed, I've never been so angry." I investigated the distance. Assuming that was her response, it implied that she had done nothing obscene with this young lady musi . Yet, I must make certain of the job musi played in my life. In the event that she wasn't a clone or an android, why did she check out at me and sound like me? Was it conceivable that I truly had a twin? Just a single method for finding out.

I looked at zeus . "We should return to the lodging. I'm eager."

The stroll back to the lodging was finished peacefully. zeus continued to gaze at me, while I just actually look at my sight. I figured I could pound every one of the pointless human feelings when I left. It worked out that something was missing, even a spot couldn't be deleted without any problem. I grew up here, so I generally sucked in. zeus grasped my hand, and I scammed it. "I told you not to contact this body," I cautioned. "One more and you will get slapped in the future."

"For what reason do you think Cairo is gone?" She asked suddenly.

"I'm not her, so I wouldn't understand what she's reasoning." I attempted to investigate musi 's memory. Since I was in her body, perhaps she could give me a clue. Doing it resembled opening an entryway in my mind. A few entryways were locked, yet one gave way to me. I saw looks at musi opening her eyes interestingly. She was in a container like specialty, and zeus was there with her. The memory vanished instantly. It wasn't in a lab, so it surely wasn't a test.

I attempted to open another entryway. This one provided me with a brief look at musi conversing with zeus . I glared. My "twin" had eyes for my lady. This could be irksome later on. I didn't leave zeus so she could track down another lady of the hour. "You understand my thought process?" I said then that the inn was approaching somewhere far off. "I think balica left you since she's accomplishing something uniquely great. Something that will benefit both of you."

"I can't envision what it is," she said.

"So let me pose you this inquiry. Will you return to your planet later on? She gestured. "Alright," I said. "Yet, you need to take balica with you. Imagine a scenario where balica constructed the land so it very well may be reasonable enough for you both to reside here. His outsider mother needed to send him here so you could both rule the earth. There could be not an obvious reason for this. If not, how could an outsider make it happen? »

"Yet, it's incomprehensible," zeus said. "Our species are not searching for planets to vanquish them. That isn't our temperament. It would be ideal for I to be aware. I was as of late delegated Sovereign of our planet, as I have previously told you."

My eyes enlarged. "Might it be said that you are the sovereign?"

"Indeed. Furthermore, balica is my better half. This implies that she ought to get back with me to our planet. We are fooling around here. The more we stay in the world, the almost certain it is that the sentinel gatekeepers will come for us. I can't remain here lengthy. I have liabilities at home."

"Furthermore, shouldn't something be said about mooner ?" I inquired. I saw looks at her in musi 's recollections. She met mooner at a certain point.

mooner is one of the central sentinel monitors who became red to think that I'm here. At the point when balica vanished when she was a child, they named her as my better half. mooner grew up realizing she would be my significant other, yet I could do without her. In my heart, there is just a single young lady, and that is you balica ." She got my hand before I could leave. "I know it's you," she murmured. "I can feel your spirit. You are my half, how would you anticipate that I should overlook something that makes me finish? »

"Let me go," I said. "I'm not her."

She dropped her hand. "This is the thing about lying. You can do it to others, however never to yourself. You know reality."

I ran before his words went through my head and harmed me. The circumstance has become more muddled. I never realized she was the Sovereign. Assuming I had gotten it done, could I have accomplished something else? I shaped my hands into clench hands. No, I wouldn't. Administering our planet was conceived. I was sent here to administer the Earth. Perhaps one day she would pick me and this planet. Any other way, we ought to be the brilliant sweethearts I've generally perused in books. There could have been no other decision.

I halted when I was before within and sucked my breath. I haven't seen him in months. Wistfulness spread to my heart. The things we have done here before have not been lost in me. I strolled in attempting to quiet my heart. Recall that you are in musi 's body, I thought. Behave like her.

The main individual I met was Jorge. She is still inconceivably gorgeous with her red hot red hair and her standard grin. Dissimilar to zeus , she wouldn't have the option to investigate my quality. As far as she might be concerned, I was musi . "For what reason do you see me like this?" She inquired. "Does Feline have a tongue? Hold up for a second, sorry I neglected you're unpracticed." I grinned at him a great deal. Presently it was the simon I knew. "Alright, you're terrifying," she said.

"How are you?" I inquired.

"We saw each other two hours prior musi . Currently inquisitive? She folded her arms before her chest. "To recap these most recent two hours, I tackled my tasks and my better half. Two hours very much spent."

diva covered my ears behind me. I could see it was her in light of her means. She generally strolled as though she needed to cheerfully hop. I heard her in any event, when she was far away. "Try not to tell that to this kid," she said. Kid, huh? From diva 's protective tone to how Simon looked regretful, it seemed like they saw musi as somebody they needed to appropriately raise. As a kid, that was the situation.

"How could you do the errands and your better half?" I requested to play. That sounds great.

Simon would have rather not botched the chance to say something, in spite of the fact that diva was there to criticize. "How about we simply say we began from the base, and afterward we're at the top." I snickered with her until zeus pulled me close by. I didn't actually hear it coming.

"Mother asks you at the gathering Jorge," zeus said. "diva , go with her."

"Indeed, captain ," simon said, welcoming. diva consciously bowed to her before they left us.

I hit my eyebrows at zeus . "Decent method for terminating everybody, my Sovereign."

"For sure." She grasped my hand and got it firmly so I was unable to give up.

"Where are we going?" I said then that she was guiding me to the lobby. She continued to drag me until we got to my old room. When inside, she moved so quick that the following time I flickered, I was lying on the bed. "No," I said as I attempted to get up.

She gave me a penetrating glare. It was the primary glare I saw coming from her. I halted and she loose. "Remain," she said. "I won't contact you." zeus continued on the bed and set down close to me. She stayed away from me, yet the other two thumbs or so could be handily mixed assuming that she wished. My heart pulsated as she shut her eyes. His eyelashes were for such a long time that I needed to contact him. "Remain like this for some time," she said. "I haven't gotten any rest since you left. I professed to make it happen, yet I really want to rest for genuine this time."

My hand floated over his face. Would it be advisable for me? Could I? I contacted her and murmured. "Then, at that point, rest," I said. "At the point when you awaken, I will constantly be there."

TO BE CONTINUE…